"Maybe I should check to see if someone's outside." She sat up on her knees, preparing to stand.

"Where are you going?" He caught her arm, holding her in place. She bit back a soft gasp as his fingers tightened on a sore place on her arm. Had she injured herself during her mad dash through the woods?

His fingers loosened and fell away. "Did I hurt you?"

"No," she said, but the burning in her arm hadn't subsided. She lifted her fingers, pressing the sore area. She felt a rip in her jacket and a sticky wetness. "I think I cut myself—"

She heard a rustling noise, then a snick. Light cut through the gloom, making her squint.

"Let me see." Rick pointed his flashlight at her arm.

Looking down, she saw a ragged furrow in the arm of her olive-drab jacket, just above the elbow. The edges were singed and damp with drying blood. She knew exactly what it was, even before Rick spoke.

"You've been shot."

PAULA GRAVES

SECRET IDENTITY

TORONTO NEW YORK LONDON
AMSTERDAM PARIS SYDNEY HAMBURG
STOCKHOLM ATHENS TOKYO MILAN MADRID
PRAGUE WARSAW BUDAPEST AUCKLAND

For my wonderful editor, Allison.
Thank you for your invaluable input and your belief in me.
I hope I live up to it.

Recycling programs for this product may not exist in your area.

ISBN-13: 978-0-373-69604-8

SECRET IDENTITY

This edition published by arrangement with Harlequin Books S.A.

For questions and comments about the quality of this book please contact us at Customer_eCare@Harlequin.ca.

www.Harlequin.com

Printed in U.S.A.

ABOUT THE AUTHOR

Alabama native Paula Graves wrote her first book, a mystery starring herself and her neighborhood friends, at the age of six. A voracious reader, Paula loves books that pair tantalizing mystery with compelling romance. When she's not reading or writing, she works as a creative director for a Birmingham advertising agency and spends time with her family and friends. She is a member of Southern Magic Romance Writers, Heart of Dixie Romance Writers and Romance Writers of America.

Paula invites readers to visit her website, www.paulagraves.com.

Books by Paula Graves

HARLEQUIN INTRIGUE

926—FORBIDDEN TERRITORY
998—FORBIDDEN TEMPTATION
1046—FORBIDDEN TOUCH
1088—COWBOY ALIBI
1183—CASE FILE: CANYON CREEK, WYOMING*
1189—CHICKASAW COUNTY CAPTIVE*
1224—ONE TOUGH MARINE*
1230—BACHELOR SHERIFF*
1272—HITCHED AND HUNTED**
1278—THE MAN FROM GOSSAMER RIDGE**
1285—COOPER VENGEANCE**
1305—MAJOR NANNY
1337—SECRET IDENTITY†

*Cooper Justice
**Cooper Justice: Cold Case Investigation
†Cooper Security

CAST OF CHARACTERS

***Amanda Caldwell*—**After suffering torture at the hands of a brutal injury, the former CIA agent has gone into hiding. But a ruthless foe has found her, and she's forced to put her life in the hands of a man she never thought she'd see again.

***Rick Cooper*—**The former security contractor knew the consequences of falling for a spy, but that hadn't made walking away from her any easier. Now his lover is in danger, and he's willing to risk his life to save her. But is he willing to risk his heart?

***Alexander Quinn*—**The CIA master spy was instrumental in tearing Rick and Amanda apart three years ago. Why is he working so hard to bring them back together?

***Jesse Cooper*—**Rick's brother owns a security agency and hired his brother after Rick's former employer, MacLear, collapsed under the weight of an international scandal. But does he have an ulterior motive for helping Rick protect Amanda?

***The Tiger*—**The man who tortured Amanda during her spy days has never been identified, much less captured. Is he behind the attempts on her life?

***Security Services Unit (SSU)*—**MacLear Security's secret unit scattered after allegations that the unit acted as a private army for a corrupt State Department official. But are some of the agents still selling their services to the highest bidder?

***Damon North*—**An undercover agent who'd once infiltrated the SSU, he's been trying to work his way back into their trust. How far is he willing to go—and who is he willing to risk—to get what he wants?

***Maddox Heller*—**The wealthy former marine seems to be working his own angle in his attempts to help Amanda. Can she and Rick trust his motives?

Prologue

Gazing across the bleak gray waters of the Tidal Basin at the Jefferson Memorial, Barton Reid tugged the lapels of his coat up to cover his exposed neck. Snow fell in halfhearted showers that mostly melted as they hit the concrete walkway extending along the bank to accommodate the tourists.

Strange to think in a few short weeks, the cherry blossoms would be in bloom. And if he played his cards right, he'd be here to watch them bloom for years to come.

Footsteps thudded toward him, too swift and determined to be a tourist's. He didn't turn right away. He didn't want to look desperate. Play it cool. Stay in control. That's how a kid from the streets of Philly had made it into the highest echelon at the Department of State. It would take those skills, and every favor he could call in, to stay out of prison.

The footsteps slowed to a stop a few feet from him. Only then did he glance down the railing to see the stocky, dark-haired man he'd contacted a day earlier.

"You're taking a chance calling me here." Salvatore Beckett had changed his look in the past couple of years, letting his dark hair grow out until it curled around the collar of his turtleneck sweater. He'd bulked up, and the definition of his muscles was obvious even through the layers of clothing he wore to ward off the mid-March cold snap.

"You know they're looking for you, yet here you are."

"I was led to understand there was a great deal of money involved."

"There is. And a favor to an old associate who may be in a position to help us in the future." He waited for Beckett to ask the obvious question, but the man just shrugged.

"You'll pay what was offered?"

"Absolutely." More accurately, his associate would come up with the exorbitant fee. Reid was merely a middleman.

"Anybody sees you with me, it's going to blow your defense."

Reid didn't have to be reminded of that troubling fact. But he had to weigh the potential for discovery against the certainty that his associate meant every word of his threat. He would connect Reid to the uprising in Kaziristan in a way that could put him in prison for the rest of his life, if he wasn't executed for treason first.

"Then let's waste no more time," Reid said aloud. "How do you feel about a trip to Tennessee?"

"Is it warmer than here?"

"I believe so."

Beckett smiled. "I'm in."

"You'll need men."

"I have them." Beckett's voice rang with confidence.

"Then here are your orders." Reid reached into the inner pocket of his coat and handed Beckett a single sheet of paper. On it were terse instructions for carrying out the job he'd just agreed to do.

Beckett's eyebrows rose slightly. "I play this my way?"

"Get it done, and you can play it any way you want."

Beckett nodded. "Nice talking to you again, Mr. Reid."

Reid turned his gaze back to the water. Along the path from the Jefferson Memorial, a young woman approached, her dark hair whipped by the icy wind into a silken halo. One hand was wrapped firmly around the hand of a little girl of three, who was laughing happily as she gazed up at the falling snow.

"Your daughter?" Beckett murmured.

Reid didn't answer.

"I'll be in touch." Beckett turned and walked slowly away.

Reid watched Meredith's approach, saw her smile as she spotted him across the distance. Anyone watching would assume he'd been waiting here for his daughter and his granddaughter.

It was mostly true.

Adrianna spotted him as they neared. Her face spread in a smile of delight that made Reid's heart crack and bleed. "Papi! Papi!" She tugged hard at her mother's hand, and Meredith let her go. Adrianna's chubby little legs churned as they ate up the distance between her and her grandfather.

He caught the little girl as she flew at him and lifted her high in the air, delighting in her giggles.

"Hello, Addie my love!" He kissed her cold cheeks and smiled at his daughter as she approached at a more leisurely pace. She was still smiling at him, but he could see the worry in her green eyes.

His life was still in flux, and unless Salvatore Beckett and his friends were able to accomplish the task he'd given them, his life was about to get more complicated still.

But he still had cards to play, even if Beckett and his men failed. He just hoped he'd never have to play them.

Chapter One

Her name wasn't really Amanda Caldwell.

She hadn't gone by her real name since she was twenty-two, fresh out of college and looking for adventure. She'd found her adventure in a very covert section of the CIA and had become a different person.

A lot of different persons.

Over the years, she'd learned never to trust a stranger—or a friend. Never sit with her back to the door. Never take the same route home twice in a row.

In a place like Thurlow Gap, Tennessee, population 224, that last rule was hard to live by. Bypassed by the major state highways, the picture-postcard mountain hamlet had never become a tourist trap like other towns bordering the Great Smoky Mountains National Park, much to the chagrin of the town's tiny chamber of commerce.

But the seclusion suited Amanda's needs very well.

Today she'd chosen a scenic route through Bridal Veil Woods behind the town's water tower. It added a few minutes to the normal ten-minute walk from town to her cottage in the foothills, but the sense of control was worth the extra time.

From the woods she emerged onto Dewberry Road two hundred yards north of the small cottage she'd bought two and a half years ago. As she headed up the road, a warbly voice called out her name. "Hey there, Miz Caldwell, did you get the job?"

Amanda turned to smile at the curly-topped little girl wobbling up to her on a bright pink bike. She'd grown up in a small town, but all the years and experiences since then had erased the memory of just how little privacy there could be in a town the size of Thurlow Gap. Everybody knew your business, even six-year-olds with scabby knees and gap-toothed grins.

"Hey there your own self, Lizzie Jean." She fell easily into the Southern accent she'd spent a couple of years losing when she joined the agency. "I did get the job."

Starting Monday, she'd be putting together the fall print ads for Gruver Hardware. It was freelance, like all the rest of the jobs she took these days, but it would pay a few months' worth of bills, sparing her from having to dip into her emergency funds.

Lizzie Hawkins slid off the bike and started walking next to Amanda. "Hey, some fella come lookin' for you earlier. He left a box on your porch. Is it your birthday or somethin'?"

Amanda kept smiling, but inside, her heart rate ratcheted up just a notch. She hadn't ordered anything, and it wasn't likely anyone in town had sent her something when they could have easily dropped it by in person.

These days, she didn't much like mysteries.

"What did the fella look like?" she asked.

"He had on a brown shirt and shorts, and he smelled sweaty." Lizzie wrinkled her nose. "He looked a little like Mr. Fielding, only a lot younger."

John Fielding was a Cherokee of indeterminate age who ran a produce stand on the edge of town. So the man who'd dropped off the package was dark-skinned and dark-haired. Maybe American Indian. Maybe…not.

Amanda's muscles tensed. Just a little. "What about his voice—anything strange about it?"

Lizzie's forehead wrinkled. "No, ma'am."

So no accent, foreign or otherwise. Maybe a local hired to deliver the package. "Did you see what he was driving?"

"A big brown truck."

Could be legit, she thought, letting herself relax a little more. Maybe someone in town had ordered her a book or something as a thank-you for a freelance design job well done.

"Thank you, Lizzie, for lettin' me know. Now you run along home, okay? I'll see you later." Amanda stayed still, watching the little girl ride away. When Lizzie was at a safe distance, Amanda turned up the gravel drive to her house. Towering pines in the front sheltered the house from the road, but as she reached the cobblestone walk to her front porch, she caught sight of the box lying on the welcome mat in front of her door.

She took the steps to the porch with care, watching for any sign of a booby trap. Not that she really thought there would be. Not after all this time.

But old habits die hard.

Official-looking labels plastered the front of the package, printed with her name and address. It was about the size of a shoe box, maybe a bit wider, with the logo of an online bookstore on the sides.

Amanda considered her options. Opening the box out here was out of the question. On the off chance it was a bomb, she'd want to limit the blast radius by putting an extra layer of protection—like walls and floors—in the way. While moving the box might be enough to set a bomb off, such a hair-trigger detonator would have made delivering the bomb dangerous. And if the detonator were remotely controlled, it probably would have gone off the minute she stepped up on the wood porch.

One thing was certain: calling the cops was out. Besides Thurlow Gap being miles from any town boasting a decent bomb squad, calling the cops because a deliveryman left a package on her porch would look nuts. She didn't need the scrutiny.

She took a deep breath and picked up the box. It was remarkably light, ruling out books. Probably ruled out a shrapnel bomb, as well, unless the shrapnel was made of something lighter than metal. Taking a quick look behind her to be sure nobody was lurking among the trees, she unlocked her front door and entered. She set the box on the hall table and locked the pair of dead bolts behind her.

The basement was the best place to open the box, she decided. It was mostly underground, with cinder-block walls that would force any explosion up rather than out toward surrounding homes.

She detoured to her bedroom and pulled a battered footlocker from her closet. Inside were some of the trappings from her former life, including body armor and a flak helmet. She strapped on the gear, grimacing at the added weight.

The sight of her reflection in the dresser mirror gave her pause. She stared at the wide-eyed woman, girded like a gladiator, and gave a soft bark of laughter. *Once a paranoid secret agent, always one.*

But she didn't take off the body armor.

Downstairs, she set the box on the floor beneath a steel worktable that had been left in the house by its former owners. She grabbed a box cutter from her jumble of a tool chest and crouched by the package, slicing a square in the side of the box and pulling out the cardboard plug.

Nothing happened.

She sat back on her heels, staring at the wad of cushioned plastic wrap poking through the hole she'd just cut. A self-conscious chuckle escaped her lips.

She sliced a bigger hole and pulled the cushioned wrap through the opening. It unfolded as it came out, revealing a small box of matches.

She set it aside and shined a flashlight through the hole in the box, checking the interior. It was just a plain box. No wires, no detonator, no C4 strapped to the cardboard anywhere.

Puzzled, she picked up the matchbox and gave it a light shake. Whatever rattled inside didn't sound like matches. She opened it slowly, waiting for something to burst free from the box, but nothing jumped out at her.

It took a second for her to realize what lay inside the box. As it registered, the box fell from her suddenly numb fingers, spilling its contents on the floor.

Artificial fingernails, painted bloodred.

Amanda flexed her hands, phantom pain skittering along the nerve endings at the tips of her fingers. She pushed back the unwanted memory and picked up the now-empty matchbox, examining it. A ten-digit number was scrawled in black ink across the inside of the box. 2565550153.

Ten digits could be a phone number, she thought. A north Alabama area code. Did she even know anyone in Alabama?

She pushed to her feet and carried the matchbox upstairs, her mind racing through all the possibilities. The fake nails she understood—whoever had sent her the box had known her in her former life, known what happened in Kaziristan. It was a calling card.

The number, though—what did the number mean?

She stopped in her room to shed the body armor and helmet, shoving them back into their closet hiding place. Dropping on the side of her bed, she contemplated the phone on her bedside table. If the number on the matchbox was a phone number, should she call it? What if it was someone trying to confirm who she really was?

She flipped the matchbox over to the blue-and-white imprint on the front. She had the same brand in her kitchen right now. Anyone could have sent it.

Something small and black in one corner caught her eye. It looked like little more than a tiny smudge, as if the ink on the box label had spattered during printing. But Amanda had seen something like it before.

She took the box to the kitchen and found a magnifying glass in the utility drawer. Under the magnifying lens, the smudge became a couple of tiny letters: A. Q.

Alexander Quinn.

Part of her wanted to pack up and leave Thurlow Gap before sunset. But the same part knew there was nowhere she could go that Quinn couldn't find her. The master spy who'd trained her in covert ops had come by the nickname "Warlock" honestly.

She might as well dial the bloody number. He already knew where she was.

KNOXVILLE, TENNESSEE, basked under an unseasonably warm late-March sun, humidity making Rick Cooper's shirt stick to his back beneath his suit jacket. He would take the jacket off but he was armed—legally, of course; over the years, he'd learned to strictly adhere to any law that didn't absolutely have to be broken. Still, no need to draw unwanted attention by sitting in an open-air bistro wearing a Walther P99 in a shoulder holster.

He checked his watch. He'd been waiting for almost an hour, but so far no one had approached his table besides the flop-haired teenage boy who kept refreshing his water glass and asking if he was ready for a menu yet. Derrick Lambert, the prospective client who'd emailed him with directions to the meeting, was apparently a no-show.

As he reached for his wallet to pay the waiter for his time, his cell phone rang. He checked the display—the call was from an unfamiliar number with a local area code. Was it his prospective client, explaining his late arrival?

He answered. "Hello?"

He heard a faint inhalation, then silence.

"Hello?" he repeated, loudly enough to draw a look from patrons at the next table.

The phone clicked dead. Rick took out his frustration on the off button and jammed his phone in his suit pocket.

"It wasn't a wrong number." The smooth voice behind Rick sent adrenaline jolting through him. He turned and gazed up into the hard hazel eyes of Alexander Quinn.

"Derrick Lambert, I presume?" Rick turned his back on the CIA spook, anger flooding his chest.

Quinn took a seat across from Rick and waved off the approaching waiter. "Sorry I'm late."

"No, you're not."

Quinn inclined his head. "Was the number blocked?"

"No."

"Good. Now, remember this. Sigurd." Quinn rose and started walking away.

Rick tossed a ten on the table and followed, falling into step as they neared the traffic light at the corner. "That's it? I wait an hour in the sun for 'Sigurd'?"

Quinn stopped and turned so quickly that Rick almost knocked into him. "Just follow the number, Cooper." The CIA agent walked away, cool and unhurried in the warm sunshine.

Bitterness rose in Rick's throat as he reversed course, striding toward the Dodge Charger parked at the curb near the bistro. Screw the phone number. Alexander Quinn had mucked up his life enough already.

He unlocked the door and slid into the hot interior of the car. The jacket went to the passenger seat, followed by his tie. Starting the car, he cranked the air up a notch, struck, not for the first time, by how good people in this country had it. Clean water. Beautiful homes. Big, shiny cars with air conditioning. He'd been in places where those luxuries would have been as out of reach as a trip to the moon.

The Charger's engine growled to life under him as he pulled out into the moderate midday traffic on Summer Street. Stopping at a red light, he pulled out his phone and punched in his brother's direct line. Jesse Cooper answered on the first ring.

"Meeting was a bust," Rick said. "I'm headed back. I'll be in the office first thing in the morning."

"Guy was a no-show?"

"He showed. But it's nothing we want to handle."

"Are you sure?" Jesse asked.

Rick's mouth tightened. "You said my experience would be an asset to Cooper Security. Do you trust it or not?"

"I trust it. You know I do. I've got to go. Isabel's back with a prospective client." Jesse hung up.

Rick looked at the cell-phone display. Pressing the back button, he took a look at the previous caller's number. It would be easy to hit Redial and see who answered, just to satisfy his curiosity.

"Sigurd," he muttered.

The traffic light turned green, forcing the issue. He laid the phone atop his jacket and accelerated through the intersection, forcing his focus back on navigating the unfamiliar Knoxville streets.

He'd been back stateside only a year now, after almost a decade in a dozen different trouble spots in the Middle East,

Africa and Central Asia. Kaziristan hadn't been the first, nor the last, but it had been the one that made him start thinking long and hard about his choice of occupations.

He was what some people would call a mercenary, though he didn't think of himself that way. He had been a private-security contractor, working for a company called MacLear Enterprises, until MacLear had gone belly up in a scandal last year—a scandal exposed by his own cousin Luke Cooper, who'd been protecting a woman being terrorized by MacLear's corrupt secret army-for-hire.

Learning the company he'd given a decade of his life to was corrupt to the bone had been a pretty hard hit for Rick's confidence. Why hadn't he seen the truth?

Had he turned a blind eye because he was too in love with the adrenaline and adventure of his job?

After the exciting life he'd led, going home to Chickasaw County again had been a daunting proposition. He'd fielded offers from other security agencies, had considered taking a few of them, but in the end, the call of home and family had proved a stronger pull than he'd anticipated.

Not that there weren't problems. A guy didn't leave his family behind and turn into a virtual ghost for ten years without creating a little interfamily tension. And he knew his brother Jesse, in particular, resented that Rick had gone with a civilian security unit rather than serving his country the way Jesse had.

Fat bit of irony, that, given that Jesse's first act upon leaving the Marines was to open his own security agency. And even Jesse couldn't deny that Rick had skills the security agency needed. He hoped in time they'd work through the old resentments and come out stronger for it.

Plus, he admired the hell out of his brother for the kind of company he was building. Cooper Security was a for-profit company, but profit wasn't the bottom line with Jesse.

He was in this work to do the kinds of jobs the government couldn't—or wouldn't—do.

Few who drove past the low-slung stucco office building on Jones Street in Maybridge knew what went on inside, what sort of men and women staffed the agency's headquarters. Most of the operatives formerly worked for an alphabet soup of U.S. government agencies—CIA, FBI, DSS, ATF, DEA, military special forces.

Most of the Cooper Security agents—even Rick—shared one thing in common: a connection to Kaziristan, a former Soviet satellite located in the midst of some of the world's hottest hot spots. Some had worked embassy security or run covert operations. Others had tracked Kaziri terrorists worldwide or interdicted their funding. His sister Megan had lost her husband in combat in Kaziristan.

For Rick, the Kaziristan connection had started with a blonde bombshell from the CIA.

IT HADN'T BEEN RICK. The voice was similar—deep and smooth, with a Southern drawl—but it couldn't belong to Rick Cooper. He was probably half a world away, tracking down suicide bombers in Karachi or running a scam on Russian mobsters—anywhere but Alabama, answering a number Alexander Quinn had put a lot of effort into sending to her. Quinn wouldn't have gone to such trouble to reunite two people he'd worked so hard to separate.

We don't fraternize with mercs. Ever.

She closed her eyes, tucking her knees to her chin. She'd always known Quinn was a manipulative bastard, but he generally had a good reason. What was his reason this time?

She looked down at the matchbox beside her on the front porch. It lay partly open, the fake nails peeking from inside, a vivid reminder of a past she wanted to bury.

Quinn knew what happened in Tablis. He'd been the first

agent to reach her after she'd escaped the rat hole where the al Adar militants had kept her for almost two weeks. He'd seen the full picture of her ordeal, painted in the rainbow hues of bruises, welts and slashes all over her body. In the bloody nubs where her fingernails had been.

She'd been overjoyed to see him that day. She'd thought the nightmare was over.

She'd been so wrong.

Tears burned her eyes like acid. She dashed them away, angry at herself for the show of weakness. Her time would be better spent trying to figure out just what Quinn was trying to tell her with the matchbox and the mysterious voice on the other end of the phone number he'd given her.

To make her earlier call, she'd used the pay phone at the gas station down the road, hoping it would offer her a semblance of anonymity. Maybe she should go back there and call the number again. Say something this time, rather than hanging up like a scared teenager too chicken to finish a prank call.

She tucked the matchbox in her pocket and started the half-mile walk to the gas station down Dewberry Road. Heat rose in shimmery waves off the blacktop, fragrant with the odor of gasoline and melting tar. The afternoon sun stung her bare arms, bringing with it a sense of déjà vu that caught her by surprise. She hadn't thought of home in a long time, of the lazy Southern summers of her childhood, when the sun couldn't get too hot or the day too long.

She'd taken a risk by choosing another tiny Southern town to escape to, but after Kaziristan and the aftermath, she'd needed that sense of familiarity. Small Southern towns were all alike in fundamental ways. Ways that made it a little easier to sleep at night.

She reached the gas station within ten minutes and pulled the matchbox from her pocket, although by now she had the number memorized, having stared at it so long before she got up the nerve to call the first time. She crossed to the phone set into the station's brick facade, sparing a glance at the lanky attendant teetering on the back legs of a metal folding chair and fanning himself with a folded piece of cardboard with a motor-oil logo peeking out of one end.

"Sure is hot for March," he muttered halfheartedly and closed his eyes, showing no signs of wanting to start a conversation.

She murmured agreement and reached for the pay phone. But before her fingers touched the receiver, it began to ring. She grabbed it on instinct. "Hello?"

There was no answer, just the sound of a car's engine. The caller must be in a car.

"Hello?" she repeated.

"Who's speaking?" a familiar voice asked.

The voice that sounded like Rick Cooper's.

Her hand trembled. "Who's calling?"

After a pause, the caller said, "Sigurd."

Amanda slammed the receiver back on the hook, the tremor in her hand spreading like wildfire to the rest of her body.

The gas station attendant looked her way, his expression mildly curious.

"Wrong number," she managed to rasp out. She wheeled and started walking away, her stride fast and purposeful.

The man's last word echoed in her head. *Sigurd.*

The phone behind her started ringing again.

"Hey, it's ringing again," the attendant called out.

She ignored him, walking faster. She heard the scrape of the attendant's chair against the cement, and a moment later, the phone stopped ringing.

She kept going, her mind racing.

If the call was a message from Quinn, it made no sense.

The CIA cut her off almost three years ago. She had no operational value to anyone, friend or foe.

Surely she'd misunderstood the caller. He'd said something else. Anything but "Sigurd."

After all, who would send an assassin after *her?*

Chapter Two

As Rick passed through Maryville, heading east, he checked his phone to make sure it was still working. He'd left a message earlier to let Jesse know about his change in plans, but so far, his brother hadn't called back for any details.

Not that Rick had any details to give him.

Thurlow Gap didn't even show up on the map he'd looked up on his phone, but the drawling local who'd answered the phone the second time gave him directions from Knoxville. He'd also shared what he knew about the woman who'd answered Rick's earlier call. She was a freelance artist named Amanda Caldwell. At least, that was the name she was going by now. But after hearing her voice on the phone, Rick knew better.

She was the woman he'd known as Tara Brady.

Tara had been a dry-witted, leggy blonde working out of the U.S. embassy in Tablis, Kaziristan. He'd been in the Kaziristan capital supporting a joint force investigating allegations of American citizens of Kaziri descent fighting with anti-government rebels north of Tablis.

Tara had never told him she was CIA, but he knew it, and she knew he knew it. It should have kept their interactions limited and circumspect—mercs and spooks didn't get involved.

But he and Tara had.

Their affair had been brief but torrid. Lingering glances led to stolen moments of intimacy, then a few nights of frantic, amazing sex in a flea-bitten hotel on the outskirts of the city. He'd never fallen for a woman so fast or so hard in his life.

But of course, it had to come to an end.

He put the memories out of his mind and concentrated on the winding drive east through the rolling foothills of the Appalachian chain. Ahead, the expansive cloud-tipped peaks of the Great Smoky Mountains National Park spread before him in hues of jade, turquoise and sapphire.

Tara loved mountains. She'd hoped one day to cross the Timrhan Mountains, the craggy, unforgiving border between Kaziristan and Russia to the north. He'd laughed at her bravado. She'd told him not to underestimate her.

That had been their last night together.

He reached the Thurlow Gap city limits around four-thirty. Though the sun was still high in the sky, nightfall hours away, the town already looked buttoned up for the evening. The gas station was still open, but the only person around was a buxom woman behind the cashier's counter near the front window.

Rick refilled the Charger's tank before approaching the woman—people often responded more openly to nosy questions if you asked them while handing them money. He added a package of cinnamon breath mints to the tab and asked her if she knew Amanda Caldwell.

"Who wants to know?" the woman asked in a whiskeyed rasp, eyeing him with a mixture of curiosity and suspicion.

"I'm an old friend. Rick Cooper."

The woman's brow creased further. "Can't say she ever mentioned you."

"She called me earlier today, but I didn't ask for her address. I was in the area so I thought I'd drop by to visit."

"She don't get many visitors."

Not surprising, Rick thought. "No significant other?"

The woman gave a loud snort. "Hell, the girl don't even have a dog keepin' her company."

He couldn't quell a glimmer of satisfaction at the woman's words, though shame followed fast on its heels. What right did he have to wish her a life of solitude? When his hand was forced, he'd chosen a mission over her. She'd made a similar choice. Things between them ended abruptly, and apparently she'd never looked back. He hadn't, either.

At least not that he'd ever let anyone see.

His coming here to talk to Tara—Amanda—wasn't personal, even now. He just wanted to know why a CIA master spy like Alexander Quinn was pulling his strings where she was concerned.

The clerk inclined her head. "Come to think of it, I reckon maybe she'd like seein' an old friend, at that. Especially a good-lookin' fella like you." Her lips quirking, she lifted a sun-leathered arm and pointed down the road. "She lives in a house a few blocks down Dewberry Road. On the left. The house is set back a bit, but you really can't miss it—she has a big black mailbox with the number 212 on it." She winked at him. "Tell her she can thank me later."

Rick smiled and thanked her, heading out to his car. As he slid behind the wheel of the Charger, his cell phone rang. It was Jesse. He considered not answering but finally thumbed the connector. "Hey, Jesse."

"Why the hell are you heading north?"

"I can't tell you that yet."

"You can't tell me?" Irritation edged his brother's drawl.

"Not yet. But it's important or I'd be on my way back to the office." Rick started the Charger.

The pause on Jesse's end was thick with annoyance. "You

may be family, but that doesn't mean you can keep pushing the envelope quite so hard, Rick."

"And you know as well as I do that some things happen we have to deal with on the q.t., Jess. This is one of them. I'll explain everything later, okay?"

Jesse sighed. "Stay in touch." He hung up.

Rick checked to see if he was safe to pull out. A black Toyota Land Cruiser turned into the gas station and pulled up at the pump behind him, leaving him in the clear.

As he waited for traffic to open up enough for him to take a left onto Dewberry Road, his gaze drifted back to the pumps, where a sandy-haired man wearing a black T-shirt and black trousers unfolded himself from the Land Cruiser and reached for the pump handle. He met Rick's glance briefly before his gaze settled on the gas pump's fuel gauge as it rang up his purchase.

Something about the sandy-haired man dinged Rick's internal radar. He didn't recognize him; Rick had a good memory for faces, and he'd never seen the man in the Toyota before. But something about him just didn't fit here in Thurlow Gap. There was a foreignness to him. As if he didn't belong.

Heading east on Dewberry Road as the clerk had directed, Rick met his own gaze in the rearview mirror. Brown eyes stared back at him under dark, quirked brows.

There's a foreignness to you, too, Rick Cooper.

He'd been away from home entirely too long.

AMANDA SCRABBLED THROUGH the closest box, cursing herself for falling into willful complacency. There was nowhere safe in the world, not even Thurlow Gap, Tennessee. No paradise was safe from murderous rage.

She should have prepared better for this moment from the second she set foot in this town.

Her former life came with baggage, but stupidly, she'd shoved that baggage into a bunch of boxes stacked haphazardly on metal shelves in her basement and told herself that she was safe enough with two dead bolts on the front door and a cheap alarm system she'd installed herself.

She'd thought the danger was over in this paradise of mountains and forests and friendly neighbors. Three years of mind-numbing normalcy had lulled her into a false sense of peace now shattered by a phone number on a matchbox and a single word spoken by a man she'd once thought she might love.

She should have had a disaster kit handy. Forget her past with the CIA; she lived within fifty miles of the Oak Ridge National Laboratory, for God's sake. She should already have been stockpiling food and water and batteries.

At least she had her savings. She'd driven to Maryville an hour ago and withdrawn all but a hundred dollars from the savings account. She had twelve grand in cash to work with. She could buy a lot of peanut butter and bottled water with money like that.

Buying a brand-new identity would be pricier, but at least she knew how to make that happen. She just had to make it to a big-enough city.

By four forty-five, she'd packed two duffel bags full of survival provisions, including two of her three handguns—the Walther P99 and the SIG Sauer P238—and nine boxes of ammo. Upstairs, her Smith & Wesson M&P 9 mm was already loaded, with an extra round in the chamber.

She'd also packed a gym bag full of underwear, jeans, T-shirts and a denim jacket. All that was left now was packing a box of nonperishable foods and she'd be ready to go.

To where, she wasn't sure.

She looped the canvas straps of the duffel bags over her arms, grunting at the weight as she started up the stairs.

As she hauled the bags through the door into the kitchen, a high-pitched beeping sound started echoing through the house. It took a second to realize what it was.

Someone had tripped her perimeter alarm.

She dropped the bags on the kitchen floor and raced down the short hallway to her bedroom. A red light on the alarm system's control panel was blinking with each beep.

She hit the code and stopped the alarm from sounding before a call went out to the local police. Whatever happened next would have to happen without putting anyone else in danger, including the local law. The good old boys who wore the uniform of Thurlow Gap's police department wouldn't be prepared for what they'd find here.

She grabbed her Smith & Wesson from the nightstand. The heft of it in her hand gave her a renewed sense of control, easing the rapid-fire cadence of her pulse. She crept down the hall to the front of the house and moved to one of the windows looking out on the shaded front yard. Sliding the curtain aside an inch, she peered out at her driveway but saw nothing.

Still, something had tripped the perimeter. Might have been an animal.

Might not.

She took a couple of deep breaths to brace herself and scooted through the doorway into the kitchen to check out the side window. But when she peeked through a space in the curtains, all she saw was movement to her right, a flash of charcoal disappearing around the side of her house, heading toward the front.

She started toward the front door, then froze when three loud raps rang through the silent house.

An assassin who knocked first?

She moved away from the door, her footfalls whisper-soft against the hardwood floor. It might be a ruse to bring her to the doorway. Even peering through the fish-eye security lens was too dangerous; any large-caliber ammunition would penetrate the wood door. Should've replaced it with a steel-reinforced one, she thought.

Should've, could've, would've. Too late now.

Knocks sounded on the door again, louder this time. She backpedaled, old instincts kicking in. She ran to the kitchen and grabbed a box of ammunition for the Smith & Wesson. Tucking the box in her waistband, she headed out the back door, hoping her visitor would keep knocking long enough for her to reach the woods behind her house. She could set up a defensive position there, her familiarity with the terrain an advantage.

She had barely reached the carport, however, when she heard the sound of footsteps coming down the flagstone walk toward the corner of the house. She raced around the back of her car and crouched behind the front fender.

The footsteps continued a moment, then fell silent. Amanda's pulse thundered in her ears. She tightened her grip on the 9 mm and held her breath, waiting for his next move.

"Tara?"

The voice, deep and familiar, sent a shiver down her spine.

"Sorry, it's Amanda now, isn't it?" Rick Cooper asked.

She remained silent.

"I know you're out here. I can feel you."

Her stomach knotted, inconvenient tears stinging her eyes.

His footsteps made a scraping sound on the concrete as he walked slowly toward her car. "I saw Alexander Quinn not two hours ago. Have you spoken with him?"

"Stop there," she commanded, pleased at the steadiness of her voice, considering how hard her heart was pounding.

He stopped.

She dared a quick peek over the hood of her car. Rick stood about ten feet away. His coffee-brown eyes met hers, his lips parting.

"You called me earlier," she said.

His mouth quirked. "Technically, you called first."

"Did Quinn tell you what to say?"

"Not exactly. You know how damned inscrutable he is."

"But he did tell you to say 'Sigurd'?"

"He told me to remember the word. *I* chose to say it."

As Quinn had known he would. Manipulative bastard. "What have you been doing since MacLear went down?"

"Working."

She sat back on her heels. "Doing what?"

"Security-threat analysis. My brother has an agency."

"I didn't know you had a brother."

"I have two of them. And three sisters. I didn't just hatch out of a rock somewhere, you know." Rick's gaze focused on the barrel of the Smith & Wesson. "I really don't like having a weapon pointed at me."

"Too bad."

He pressed his lips in a tight line. "Very well. What does 'Sigurd' mean?"

"Nothing." She motioned with the gun. "I need to leave. You're standing in front of my car."

"What does 'Sigurd' mean?" he repeated.

Before she could answer, something hit her windshield with a loud crack, spider-webbing the glass.

"Get down!" she shouted to Rick.

She heard a soft thud and a low groan.

"Rick?"

Scrabbling sounds came from the other side of the car, moving toward her. She wheeled and aimed the Smith & Wesson at the sound. Rick ducked around the front of the car, tumbling forward onto his hands and knees at the sight of the gun. "May I please hide behind your car?" he gritted between his teeth.

She made room for him. "Are you hit?"

"Grazed my arm, I think. Sigurd, I presume?"

"Sigurd's a warning, not a person." She risked a quick peek over the hood of her car. She saw a flash of black move between the pines in her front yard. "There's someone in the front yard. Dressed in black."

Rick crouched beside her, looking through the car windows. He took a hissing intake of breath as a black-clad figure slipped one tree nearer.

"Is there a way out of here?"

"We can escape into the woods, but I'm guessing whoever's out there isn't alone."

"I'm not so sure." Rick told her about a stranger he'd spotted at the gas station. "He was definitely alone, and I'm pretty sure the man in black out there is the same guy."

"How can you tell? He's wearing a ski mask."

"Same body build, same clothes. If you spot a Toyota Land Cruiser nearby—"

Amanda peered over the hood of the car. The man in black was on the move again, slipping out into open. For the hell of it, Amanda fired off a couple of quick shots in his general direction, the gunfire echoing in the surrounding woods.

"Don't waste the ammo," Rick warned. "We'll need it."

"What we really need is a vehicle. We can't hike out of these woods." She looked at Rick, her heart giving a small leap as she realized his face was only inches away.

For a moment, the rest of the world seemed to disappear, and she was back in Tablis, her body tangled with his, hot and straining for more—more pleasure, more closeness, more communion. But the crackle of footsteps on the dry leaves in her yard dragged her back to the present, a sobering reminder that there were damned good reasons not to let herself get wrapped up in anyone again.

"Let me lead him away," Rick suggested. "You can take the car and get out of here."

"And leave you to die?" She shook her head. "No way in hell. I don't leave a man behind."

He gave her a quizzical look, and she dropped her gaze, hiding the chaos of emotion churning in her chest. He probably had no idea what had happened to her the day after they ended their affair. The CIA never publicized its casualties.

"We can't wait here for him to reach us."

"In my kitchen is a duffel bag. I packed it to run. I'm going around the back and out into the woods. I'll lure him away from here. Where's your car?"

"Parked down the road."

"He may have seen it—and if he disabled it—"

"I hid it off the road. Didn't want it stolen."

"Take the duffel. Go to your car and drive a mile east. I'll meet you if I make it."

There was a pained look in his eyes as his gaze met hers. "No ifs," he said fiercely. "You make it or else."

She fought against a sudden flood of weakness. Where had he been when she was rotting in a Kaziri rebel prison, wondering if anyone remembered her at all?

You're the one who started pushing him away.

But he was the one who'd spoken the final words.

"Wait for me to draw his fire away from here, then go inside. There's a first-aid kit in the duffel, but I don't think you'll have time to waste."

He moved suddenly, cupping the back of her neck and pulling her to him. "If you can kill him, do." He kissed her forehead.

Swallowing hard, she scooted backward, losing cover for

just a moment. No gunfire came her way, to her relief. She must have caught the attacker changing positions.

She edged her way around the side of the house, straining for any sound ahead. Her house butted up to a bluff, offering little room to maneuver. But if she could get around to the other side of the house, the woods spread for almost three miles to the east. She knew Bridal Veil Woods like the back of her hand. If she could get a head start into the cover of the trees, she could outmaneuver the gunman and get away.

Or get the drop on him.

RICK'S ARM WAS HURTING like a son of a bitch, but the wound was superficial, a bloody graze on his upper left arm that would require some first aid once he had a chance to breathe again but wasn't likely to cause him any real problems. He found the duffel bag in the kitchen, lying on the floor where she'd left it, probably when he knocked on her door unexpectedly.

He wasn't sure why Tara—Amanda—was hiding out in the middle of Nowhere, Tennessee, but something had gone terribly wrong since the last time he'd seen her. He'd seen it in her haunted blue eyes.

What had the CIA done to her?

He hauled the duffel bag over one shoulder and headed to the back door, waiting for the bark of her Smith & Wesson to the east, his signal to make a run for it.

When the gunfire came, it was a pair of shots. One impossibly close, the other from the woods to the right of the house.

Then silence.

Rick froze in place, not sure what to do next. After a beat, he heard footfalls on the front porch, slow but steady.

He leveled his Walther at the door, his heart pounding a

familiar, rapid-fire cadence. He'd been away from war zones a year now, but some things a man never forgot.

"Rick, it's me." Amanda's voice came through the thin wooden door. "I'm unlocking the door and coming in. Please don't shoot me."

He kept the Walther steady, aware she could be speaking at the point of a gun.

There was a rattle of the doorknob, the slide of a key into the lock and the scrape of the dead bolt disengaging. The door swung open and Amanda entered alone, looking pale and jittery. "I shot him. He's dead," she said. "I need you to see if he's the man you remember from the gas station."

He laid a comforting hand on her arm when he reached her side. Her muscles twitched at his touch, as if she was ready to bolt at any second. Probably was—it was hard to control the physiological instinct for fight or flight, even if you were a highly trained intelligence officer.

The body of the shooter lay on the grass in front of her yard, blood still oozing from a chest shot. "Good aim," he murmured, circling the body to get a look at the man's face.

What he saw there came as a complete surprise.

"It's not the guy from the Land Cruiser," he said aloud, his voice tight and strained.

"But you recognize him?" she asked.

He nodded. "His name is Delman Riggs." He looked up at her, his heart in his throat. "He used to work for MacLear."

Chapter Three

"We have to move his body." Amanda kept her voice low and calm, even though an endless shriek of terror played in a constant loop in her mind, echoing the memories that would never leave her as long as she lived.

But she had to focus on what needed to be done now. She could fall apart later, when she was finally alone again.

Rick's eyes narrowed. "Move his body where?"

"I don't care," she said. "It doesn't matter. We have about five minutes before the police get here. My neighbors will call in the gunfire. We've got to move now."

"Why don't we stick around and talk to the cops." Rick spoke to her in a careful voice, as if he realized how close she was to snapping. "We'll tell them what happened. I have the wound to prove we were under fire."

She stared at him. "The Thurlow Gap cops aren't cut out for a mess like this. Do you honestly think this will be the only attempt on my life?" She checked the Smith & Wesson's clip to make sure she'd fired only four shots in the chaos. God knew how many more rounds she might need before this nightmare was over. "We're wasting time talking about this."

Rick stared at her. She saw the moment he realized she was right, that they couldn't stay here and wait for the cops. But it was clear from his expression that he didn't want to bug out. He wanted to handle this mess the normal way—call the cops, make a report, then forget about it and go on with life.

Good for him. She was glad he'd found his own little dose of normal in the world.

But she never would.

Sliding the pistol into the waistband of her jeans, she headed up the porch steps. "If you want to talk to the locals, fine. Stay here and chat it out with them. I have to go." She went into the house, picked up the duffel bag Rick had left just inside and carried it out to the porch.

"How are you getting out of here? You think they won't put out an APB for your car?" Rick asked from the bottom of the steps as she descended.

"I'll walk." She slung the heavy duffel bag over her shoulder, looping her arm through the canvas strap.

"And get picked up before you reach the next county." Rick shook his head, falling in step with her as she headed toward the woods. "I'll drive you wherever you want to go."

She stopped at the edge of the clearing, taking a good look at him. The past three years had been kinder to him than her. He'd always been good-looking, but the intervening years had added lines of maturity to his face that suited him. His dark eyes looked older, too. Wiser, maybe. A lot more jaded.

She could sympathize with that.

"I don't know where I want to go," she admitted. "I just want to get out of here before the people around here end up getting hurt. They don't deserve this kind of mess. And I'm not ready to offer myself up as a sacrificial lamb."

"There's going to be a mess, no matter what we do," Rick warned. "If you disappear, no warning, no goodbyes, and the cops come here and find bullet holes riddling your carport—"

"All right! You're right. There's going to be a mess." A manic energy bubbled in her chest, driving her relentlessly toward desperation. "So let's make it a big mess."

Reversing course, she jogged around to the back of the cabin, where she kept the gasoline generator that had gotten her through one frigid winter when the mountain snowfall had knocked out her electricity. Next to the generator stood the weatherproof bin where she kept a five-gallon container of gasoline. She'd just stocked up a couple of days earlier, in anticipation of next week's promised thunderstorms.

She didn't like to be stuck in the dark. Not anymore.

Rick caught up with her. "What are you doing?"

Amanda pulled the gas can from the bin and pulled off the cap. The pungent odor of gasoline fumes wafted around her, fueling her sense that she'd reached a point of no return. She met Rick's troubled gaze, her lips curving in a ghost of a smile. "Remember Choqori?"

His eyes widened. "You're not going to—"

"Burn it to the ground?" A ripple of laughter escaped her throat. It sounded like madness. "Oh, yes. Yes, I am."

WITHIN TEN MINUTES, they'd made it through the woods undetected and headed out of Thurlow Gap, driving south, leaving behind one hell of a bonfire. They'd already heard sirens heading for Amanda's property, which meant the fire would be put out sooner or later. And, eventually, people would probably be seeking Amanda for questioning about the charred body inside.

But they could worry about that problem another day, Rick thought as he tore off a piece of his shredded shirtsleeve to get a better look at the bloody groove in his upper arm. He grimaced at the sight of the torn and friction-burned skin.

"It's not as bad as it looks," Amanda said from her position behind the steering wheel. She was keeping to the speed limit—not too fast, not too slow—although Rick could see a frenetic glow in her smoky-blue eyes that suggested it was taking all of her willpower to keep from gunning the Charger up the highway.

"I need to clean it out before infection sets in." There were pieces of singed shirt and probably pieces of bullet shrapnel embedded in the groove of flesh, rendering the wound a fertile environment for bacteria.

"As soon as you drop me off in Chattanooga, you can go find a doctor."

He shot her a look. Drop her off? Did she really think that was going to happen? "Doctors have to report gunshot wounds. You know that."

She shrugged. "Tell him you gouged it on a nail."

"There's not a nail in the world big enough to make this kind of wound."

"Then tell him it was a railroad spike."

He clenched his jaw, pain from the gunshot wound exacerbating his growing frustration. "How about this instead? We find somewhere outside Chattanooga to hunker down for the night, and you help me bandage up the gunshot wound I got trying to help you while *we* figure out what to do next."

She slowed the Charger as they came up to a traffic light, taking advantage of the wait to look at him. The fiery determination evident in the set of her square jaw was so familiar it made his chest ache. She had always been the most stubborn creature he'd ever known.

"There's no we, Rick. You never should have come here. We're going to pretend that you didn't."

"You were always better at pretending than I was."

The look she gave him held a hint of hurt. Just a hint, as if the life she'd lived since they'd last said goodbye had mostly cauterized whatever wound had remained from their breakup.

He wished he'd been able to rid himself of the painful memories as efficiently as she had. She still haunted him, usually deep in the night when he was alone and pondering the mess his life had become since that day when he walked away from her for what he thought would be forever.

"It's one night, Tara—"

"Amanda," she said sharply. "Tara Brady's dead. She's not coming back."

He clamped his mouth shut, then started again. "Amanda. Just one night."

"I never did tell you my real name, did I?"

He shook his head.

"I guess it won't hurt now. It was Audrey. Audrey Scott."

"From somewhere in south Mississippi," he murmured.

She slanted another look at him. "What makes you think that, hotshot?"

"In Kaziristan, you had your accent almost completely contained," he said, pleased that he'd managed to surprise her. "But you've been living in Tennessee for a while now, surrounded by people who talk a lot like the people from where you grew up. Your accent has come out to play again."

She pressed her lips into a tight line. When she spoke again, that subtle hint of Mississippi had been ruthlessly stripped away. "I won't make that mistake again."

"I like the accent," he admitted. He'd heard it now and then, back when they were sneaking moments of passion in a Kaziristan hotel. When she'd started to lose control, her Mississippi accent had slipped out more than once. "It's sexy."

The look she shot his way would have been lethal if it had been a bullet.

Before he got a chance to enjoy his small victory, Amanda released a soft curse.

"What?"

"There's a police cruiser about a quarter mile back. Coming up fast." She spoke in a flat, grim tone.

Rick's gut tightened, but he'd been trained by MacLear to keep his head in a threatening situation. He imagined her CIA training had been even better preparation.

"Let's determine one thing right now," he said, fighting to keep the punch of adrenaline out of his voice. "No cops get shot, no matter what happens. If we have to talk our way through the truth, it's better than killing a cop."

She grimaced at him. "What do you think I am?"

"A burned CIA agent without much to lose."

"Technically, I wasn't burned. I was relieved of duty. They didn't cut me off completely." Her voice didn't hold a lot of conviction, Rick noticed.

"Just keep doing what you're doing. Stay in the right lane and keep to the speed limit." He pulled his jacket back on, hoping the bloody rip in the dark leather wouldn't catch the policeman's eye if he pulled them over.

The cruiser approached in the side mirror, moving at a clip. Rick resisted the urge to turn and look out the back windshield. Talk about drawing attention to them—

"He's passing us," Amanda murmured.

Rick kept his gaze straight ahead, ignoring the police cruiser until it passed. He allowed himself to breathe again.

"One threat averted," Amanda said. "It won't be the last."

"You really have no idea who'd be gunning for you?"

"I have no idea who'd think I'm significant enough to pay for a hit."

Rick leaned his head back against the headrest, trying to think his way through the chaotic mess of the past three hours. It had started, for him, with the phone call to Cooper

Security from Alexander Quinn claiming to be Derrick Lambert and wanting a meeting in Knoxville. Clearly, he'd wanted Rick to be in the area when Amanda called.

He'd known Rick would recognize the voice. He'd known he couldn't walk away without trying to see her.

"You called me. Where did you get the number?" he asked aloud, rolling his head to the side so he could look at her.

She slanted a quick look his way. "Someone left a package on my front steps. Your number was inside the package."

"Just my number?"

"Mostly. You know me. Curious as a cat."

Cautious as a mouse was more like it, he thought. At least these days. "So Quinn sent you my number, and he arranged for me to be within an hour's drive from where you lived."

"Looks that way," she said carefully.

"And he pretty much put me in a position to deliver a warning to you. But why me? Why didn't he give it to you himself?"

Her lips curved a little, making his breath catch. Time had given her a lean, feral look she hadn't possessed when he'd known her three years ago, but when she smiled, he saw the ghost of the vibrant, fearless woman he'd spent a few glorious months loving in the heart of a war zone.

"Why does Alexander Quinn do anything he does?" She shook her head. "Foreign services around the globe have written books trying to answer that question."

Rick gazed through the windshield, wincing at the growing ache in his arm where the bullet had grazed him. According to the highway sign they'd just passed, they were near Athens, Tennessee, about an hour outside Chattanooga. Once they reached the city, they could find some nondescript little no-tell motel off the highway and hunker down for a night. Clean up his wound and maybe plot their next move.

"When we get to Chattanooga, I should call my brother."

She shot him a look of disbelief. "We're not contacting anyone, Rick. We have no way of knowing whether or not Quinn sent that gunman after me. And since he's the one who sent you, he probably has your family's phones tapped."

Her level of paranoia was off the charts. "But why would Quinn send me to Thurlow Gap to warn you if he was in on the assassination attempt?"

"I don't know!" Her voice rose, tinged with fear. He stared at her, barely recognizing her as the woman he'd last seen on a street in Tablis, Kaziristan, walking away with long, confident strides, each click of her high heels against the cobblestone street ripping another shred in his heart.

Tara Brady had been brazen in her sense of control and self-reliance. She'd needed nobody.

Not even him.

Amanda Caldwell, on the other hand, might share Tara's honey-blond hair and smoky-blue eyes, but the confidence came and went. Back at the house, with the gunman breathing down their necks, she'd been all business, her training taking over with a vengeance. But now that the adrenaline rush had faded, and they were driving into an unknown future, the fear he'd seen lurking earlier behind her eyes had crept to the surface.

She was terrified, and seeing her that way was more frightening to Rick than being shot at, back at her cabin.

"Why did you leave the CIA?" he asked. She hadn't yet given him a satisfying answer to that question, had she?

He saw her jaw set like concrete. "Got tired of it."

"Just like that?"

"Sure. Why not?"

"I asked questions about you. Back in Kaziristan." After the debacle that had been the beginning of the end of his career with MacLear.

Losing Amahl Dubrov to the terrorists had been the worst error he'd ever made on the job. God only knew what the al Adar rebels had done to Dubrov once they got their hands on him.

Rick never should have listened to Salvatore Beckett. He should have trusted his instincts and bugged out of Tablis with Dubrov before al Adar found them.

"Asked questions?" Amanda said when he didn't continue.

He'd wanted to see her one more time before he headed back stateside, he remembered. He had been due back in Atlanta the next evening to attend a debriefing with Jackson Melville, MacLear's CEO. Melville wouldn't be pleased. Rick had known losing Dubrov might cost him his job. "It was a few weeks after we last met. I was heading back to the States. I just wanted to see you one more time before I went."

Her expression closed like a door. "I wasn't in Tablis anymore. You wouldn't have been able to find me."

"Nobody had any answers for me. So I left."

Her gaze focused on the road ahead. She said nothing else.

He sank back against the seat, resting his head against the window. In the side mirror, traffic behind him was as light as it was on the road in front of them. They'd hit the road at just the right time—

In the mirror, a vehicle that had been just a dot on the road behind them had grown several sizes larger in the span of the few seconds his gaze had settled on the mirror.

Next to him, Amanda uttered another low oath. He looked up to find her staring at the rearview mirror, her brow furrowed. "Vehicle, coming up fast."

"I know." He checked the side mirror again and saw the black dot was a large black SUV bearing down on them, moving at alarming speed. It looked familiar. "I think that's the Toyota Land Cruiser I saw at the gas station back in Thurlow Gap."

"Great," she muttered tersely.

He pulled his Walther from the holster at his waist and checked the clip. He'd transferred a couple of boxes of ammunition for the Walther from the trunk of the Charger to his glove compartment before they hit the road, and he'd seen extra guns and rounds in Amanda's duffel bag, as well. But if the person in the fast-approaching SUV had backup and bigger weapons, all their firepower might not be enough.

"If they're up to no good, I don't think we can shoot this thing out," Amanda said.

"How are your defensive-driving skills?"

"Rusty," she admitted, "but I still remember a few things."

Rick checked the back window. The SUV was about four car lengths back. "This Charger will do 140 miles an hour. I bet we can outgun that land boat back there. If they try to run us off the road or start shooting, just floor it."

She gave a brisk nod, her gaze flicking back and forth between the light traffic ahead and the rearview window. He saw her shoulders tighten. "Weapon!" she barked.

He turned and saw a large-caliber handgun extending from the passenger window of the Toyota. "Duck and gun it!"

Dropping low in his seat, he held on as the Charger bolted forward, the engine singing with the power surge, and sent up a quick prayer of thanks that his sister Shannon had talked him into buying the muscle car instead of a less expensive, more practical sedan.

Amanda weaved the Charger through traffic, the SUV staying with her for about a mile before it started to fall back.

"I love this car," she declared, sounding like the Tara

Brady he remembered. A rush of pure male hunger surged through him, badly timed but strangely welcome. For the first time in a long time, he felt like the Rick Cooper who'd fallen hard for the sexy American spook.

It was about damn time.

Chapter Four

At least it wasn't a tent in the Sudan, Amanda thought as she surveyed the shabby facade of the roadside motel a few miles outside Chattanooga. After the scare on the interstate, they'd taken side roads and backtracked now and then, which turned their hour's drive to Chattanooga into five long and tension-filled hours.

"Floozy up, pretty mama." Rick straightened his jacket, grimacing with pain as the leather rubbed his wounded arm. He unbuttoned a couple of buttons on his shirt, glancing at her. "Come on, if we're going to sell this one-night stand, you're going to have to look a little trampier."

She slanted a look his way, not missing the gleam of amusement in his eyes. He was enjoying himself, the jerk. She wanted to be angry at him, mostly because anger was a lot easier to deal with than what she was really starting to feel, a flicker of the old excitement that used to grip her right in the chest every time she spotted him coming her way.

Their time together had been so long ago. So much had happened since then. Things he didn't know about. Things she didn't want to remember.

It's a job, she reminded herself. If anyone in the world knew how to become someone she wasn't, it was the little girl born in McComb, Mississippi, who'd hidden from her series of drunk "daddies" and browbeaten mama by pretending to be someone—anyone—she wasn't. She pushed her jeans down around her hips and started to pull up her T-shirt to tie it into a knot over her belly, stopping just in time.

She shot another quick look at Rick to see if he'd noticed her sudden hesitation. He was scanning the area outside the car, making sure they hadn't picked up a tail somewhere along the detour route.

She tucked the shirt into her jeans, hiding the scars across her lower back where the al Adar rebels had made her pay for her insolence. Exposed midriff was out. She'd just have to go the more obvious route. "Do you have a knife handy?" Hers was packed in the duffel bag.

Rick pulled a Swiss Army knife from his pocket and handed it to her with a curious look. "Is this about to get kinky?"

She opened the sharpest blade and sliced through the neckband of her T-shirt, tearing the fabric down the front until the tops of her breasts, cradled in a lacy blue bra, were exposed. She glanced his way. "Trampy enough?"

His gaze settled on her breasts. The air between them felt like a furnace blast, thick with heat and tension.

"That'll do." He cleared his throat and looked away.

The manager's office was a tiny room at one end of the one-story motel. Just outside, Rick threw his good arm around her shoulders, tugging her close to his side. An overwhelming sense of familiarity rocked her, sending a tremble through her legs. He was hard and lean-muscled, masculine to the core despite his outer veneer of sophistication. She'd always known there was a hard-loving, hard-fighting Alabama country boy lurking beneath the surface of the urbane charmer.

It was one of the things she'd loved most about him.

At the front desk, a balding man in his early fifties sat behind the counter, reading a Zane Grey novel. *Knights of the Range.* One of her favorites. He didn't look up immediately.

Rick caught her chin in his hand, drawing her face up to his. As his lips descended, she felt like a fly trapped in a web, watching the spider's inexorable approach.

His lips met hers. Soft at first, then fierce and hard, as if fueled by an impatient hunger he was desperate to sate. The world around her reeled, forcing her to clutch him with both hands to stay upright.

He dragged his lips away and turned to look at the desk clerk. He'd finally looked up from his book at their public display of hormones.

"One hour, two hours or the night?" he asked, his gaze dropping to Amanda's breasts.

"The night," Rick answered, bending his head to suckle the skin at the base of her neck. Electricity shot through her, heading straight for her sex. Her knees wobbled again.

"That'll be forty bucks. Phone and TV extra."

Rick licked the curve of her collarbone, his tongue rough-textured and hot. Heat settled low in her belly as his voice rumbled through her. "All we need is a bed."

The clerk laughed, his gaze still firmly affixed to the front of Amanda's ripped T-shirt. Rick pulled his lips away from her neck long enough to hand the clerk two twenties and retrieve the key the man handed him.

He walked outside with his arm still around Amanda's shoulders. She knew, as they moved down the breezeway toward the room, that she should move away from him, but her body wouldn't listen to the warning bells clanging in her head.

Rick handed her the key when they reached the room. As she unlocked the door, her hands trembled violently. She tried to tell herself it was delayed reaction from the day's events, but that attempt at self-delusion didn't last past the first step inside the motel room, when Rick slammed the door shut behind them and flattened her against it with a hungry growl.

His mouth descended, hot and fierce against hers. Twining his hands with hers, he pressed them against the door, pinning her in place for his slow, thorough exploration of her mouth.

He felt so familiar she ached, but there was also a newness to his touch, as if he were an entirely different person from the man she'd taken willingly to her bed a few short years ago. The contradictory sensation was both exciting and disconcerting, setting her pulse racing.

His hips pressed against hers, the hard ridge of his sex pushing into the softness between her thighs until she was aflame with anticipation. The denim between them was too much. She needed to feel the hot silk of his skin on hers, creating friction and fire.

She pulled one hand from his grasp and reached between them, cupping his sex in her palm. His breath burning against her lips, he growled a low profanity that only spurred her to stroke him more firmly.

Her body prickled all over, like a deadened limb coming slowly, painfully to life. When he dipped his head to taste the swell of her breast peeking over the edge of her bra, her body hummed with delight.

He reached for the hem of her T-shirt and tugged upward. The soft cotton rasped against the scar tissue crisscrossing her back.

Ice replaced fire, freezing her in place. Rick didn't seem to notice at first, sliding his hand under the loose cotton to trace the curve of her lower spine.

But as his fingers crept closer to the web of scars across her back, she grabbed his wrists and tugged his hands away from her back. "No."

He took a faltering step backward. “What?”

“No,” she said more firmly, her skin crawling where the scar tissue gathered. There were other scars, more than just the ones on her back.

The al Adar rebels had not been gentle.

He walked away from her, toward the lone window in the tiny bedroom. “I’m sorry.”

“No,” she said again, her tone apologetic. “I just—I can’t go back.” For so many reasons.

He flexed his injured arm, frowning with pain. “Okay.”

“We’re supposed to be fixing your arm,” she said gruffly.

“I think I need a shower first.” He waved toward the door. “Think you could get the supplies out of the Charger?”

“Of course.” She headed outside and took their bags from the car. When she returned, the shower was running in the bathroom. She dropped the bags by the door and sat on the end of the bed, trying not to look too closely at the faded, threadbare bedspread.

She and Rick would have to share that bed tonight, after what had almost happened between them a few minutes ago.

How on earth were they going to get through the night?

Rick emerged from the bathroom wearing only his jeans and a towel wrapped around his neck. He gave her a wary look as he approached the bed, his eyes dark and pained. “I think I cleaned most of the grime out of the wound,” he rasped.

She felt an instant twinge of sympathy. “Sit here and I’ll bandage you up.”

While he settled on the end of the bed, she dug through her duffel bag for the first-aid kit. Gathering the supplies she needed and returning to his side, she got to work.

“If we can keep ointment and bandages on it for the next few days, you ought to be able to avoid infection.” Her voice came out in a tremble, but her hands, at least, remained steady as she dabbed a generous layer of antibiotic ointment across the bloody gouge in his upper arm. She flattened a thick gauze pad over the wound and taped it down. "There we go."

He caught her hand as she started to back away. "I really am sorry about before. I took the charade too far."

A dart of pain hit its mark just beneath her breastbone. "Yeah. The charade. Just like old times, huh?"

"It wasn't a charade back then," he murmured.

"Sometimes it was," she countered, keeping her voice deliberately light. "That was the fun of it."

His lips curved slightly. "Sometimes," he conceded.

She took her time gathering up the supplies and putting them back into the first-aid kit, needing that little bit of distance to get her emotions back under steely control.

"Maybe we should have paid extra for the phone," Rick commented as she was putting the kit back into her duffel bag.

"Thinking of ordering a pizza?" she asked over her shoulder, pleased with the easy tone of her voice.

"I am kind of hungry," he admitted.

She pulled a couple of protein bars out of her duffel bag and tossed him one. *"Bon appétit."*

He caught it, shooting her a wry grin. *"Merci."*

Not trusting herself to sit on the bed beside him, she settled cross-legged on the floor at the end of the bed and unwrapped her own protein bar.

"But what I meant about the phone was, I think I should call my brother Jesse."

Her gaze snapped up, meeting his. "No."

"Whoever's after you probably doesn't know or care who I am. They may not even know about me at all. They're certainly not going to know to tap the phone of a no-tell motel room in the middle of Nowhere, Tennessee. And they won't know my brother Jesse from Adam."

"We don't know how that guy found me in the first place," she argued. "Or how the men on the highway tracked us down."

"I checked my car for a tracker back at the gas station outside Athens," Rick assured her. "And we looked at our bags, too, just in case—"

"You don't survive in this business if you take stupid chances," she said flatly. "Calling someone—at this stage of the game, at least—would be very stupid."

"It's not a game, Tara." He clamped his mouth to a tight line before correcting himself. "Amanda. You're not on a mission. Your life is in danger, and you don't have to worry about breaking cover this time."

"Oh, but I do," she answered, realizing in that moment just how much she hated the truth. It hadn't taken very long after she'd stepped into the spy game to realize there would be only two ways out when she was done. She could quit the CIA and make a concerted effort to be so famous an expert on the agency that killing her would be more trouble than it was worth—or she could live the rest of her life under the radar. As a covert operative who'd crossed a lot of dangerous people, she didn't have any other viable options if she wanted to survive.

She'd chosen the latter, especially after the ordeal in Kaziristan. All she wanted to do was hide from the world as long as she could afford to.

"Why aren't you using your real name?" Rick asked carefully, as if he knew what a volatile question he was asking.

"Because I haven't been Audrey Scott for so long, I don't know how to be her anymore." She knew the reply seemed flippant and nonsensical, but it was true. The little girl from Mississippi had lived a long, hard life before she escaped on a scholarship to college and met the CIA recruiter who'd changed her life. Even if it were safe to return to her old life, she wouldn't want to do it.

Some things were worse than living a lie.

His watchful gaze felt intrusive, forcing her to look away. She knew he had questions about her past. He'd always had questions, though he'd never asked them again after her light rebuff of his first queries so long ago. Still, she'd seen the curiosity in his eyes, even in the throes of passion. He wanted to know who she was. All of who she was.

She just couldn't share that much of herself with Rick.

Not with anyone.

"Okay," he said finally, breaking the uncomfortable silence that had fallen between them like a wall. "No phone calls."

She looked up, grateful for his concession. But she saw determination lurking in his eyes.

"Yet," he added.

She held his gaze, an idea forming at the back of her mind, driven into hiding by Rick's relentless scrutiny. "I *am* hungry," she admitted quietly, careful to keep her voice or expression from revealing even a hint of what she was planning. "That protein bar didn't do the trick. You know, I saw a burger joint down the road, just before we reached here. Could you run back there and pick up some food for us while I take a shower?"

He seemed surprised by the sudden change of topic. "Sure. What would you like?"

"A burger and some fries will be great." Her mouth watered at the thought of the meal she wouldn't get to eat.

Because she didn't plan to be around when he got back.

IT TOOK A MOMENT, upon scanning the empty interior of the motel room, for Rick to realize he'd been well and truly had.

A faint flutter of hope propelled him into the bathroom to make sure she wasn't there, but the bathroom was just as he'd left it, towels still damp from his shower, lying on the sink where he'd put them. There was no sign that she'd taken a shower of her own.

She'd ditched him. Probably why she'd sent him out for food in the first place—even as he'd obeyed his growling stomach's order to do what she said without asking questions, he'd thought her reversal a bit strange. He just hadn't wanted to push her too hard, one way or another.

He should have known better. It wasn't the first time a woman had walked out of his life and left him wondering why.

He went to retrieve a small survival kit from his bag but found it was missing. So was one of the two boxes of 9 mm rounds he'd packed for the trip. She'd left one for him, he noted.

No matter. He had extra rounds stored in the trunk of the Charger, plus an extra survival kit.

He threw everything into his bag and carried it out to the Charger. Retrieving the box of extra rounds, he dumped about twenty into the outside pocket of the survival kit stored in his trunk and strapped the kit to his belt. The cooling food went in the passenger seat. If they had to make a quick getaway when he found her and dragged her back here—fighting the whole way, no doubt—at least they'd have food for the trip.

The motel was just off a busy county highway, but behind the building was nothing but wooded wilderness, stretching as far as he could see. No way would she risk traveling on the highway. She'd head into the woods, probably figuring she could escape him more easily that way. And she'd be harder to spot for anyone who'd followed them this far, too.

Probably thought she was pretty smart, he mused blackly

as he looked for the most obvious entry into the woods. Thought she'd outwit the dumb merc by sending him off on a diversion.

A smile curved his lips as he saw signs of her escape imprinted on the bushes and underbrush she'd run through. At most, she was ten minutes ahead of him—maybe less, since she'd stopped to steal his supplies first. Her duffel bag would slow her down, too.

He started to head right after her, then considered the possibility that she was setting up a diversion to lure him into the woods so she could hotwire the Charger and make her getaway.

That wasn't going to happen. He got back into the car and drove it about a hundred yards down the road, concealing it behind a scrubby stand of elderberry bushes that grew along the shoulder of the highway. He added extra branches as camouflage, then hurried back to follow Amanda from the place where she'd started out.

She'd tried to keep to a random, twisting route, he saw as he followed her trail, sometimes circling back but always moving southeast, toward the Georgia line. Because they were on Lookout Mountain, the terrain was hilly and boulder-strewn, making for a difficult walk.

He'd lost some blood and strength from the bullet wound, but the shower and the protein bar had done a lot to lift his flagging energy. Plus, he had a wellspring of irritation driving him forward.

Leaving was always her answer, wasn't it? It didn't really matter that he'd been the one to say the words that drove the final nail in their relationship. She'd been saying them in her actions for weeks. They'd both known their relationship would eventually catch the attention of their superiors. She worked with spooks, and his bosses weren't much less omniscient. He'd received the first warning, and while he'd loved the work he was doing at the time, he would have chucked the whole thing to be with her.

But only if she'd felt the same way.

And clearly, she hadn't.

Just like now, she'd run away from him the second things got complicated. Not so obviously then as now, but the signs had been strong enough to force Rick to stay silent about wanting to choose her over the job.

She'd started begging off their planned assignations. Made excuses not to be anywhere near him. And when she admitted that her superiors had told her to end the relationship or else, he'd seen clearly she had no intention of leaving the CIA for him.

So he'd ended things for them both.

He'd regretted that choice every day since. He knew she'd loved him. But leaving the CIA was harder than leaving MacLear. There were more consequences. Far more danger.

He'd expected her to make the same choice he had just as easily as he'd made it. That hadn't been fair.

What if he'd given up on them too soon?

Maybe following her into the wilderness like this was a fool's errand. Maybe there was nothing left of the woman he'd loved so much, nothing left to hope for.

But he wouldn't know until he caught up with her, would he? This time, he wasn't going to let her go without a fight.

AMANDA CONSULTED THE compass Rick had helpfully packed in a small survival kit in his suitcase. She was still heading southeast, though more slowly than she'd have liked. After the first mile, she'd stopped backtracking, feeling fairly safe that she'd have lost any pursuer after that first stretch of woods. Now it was just a matter of finding civilization again, hopefully before nightfall, and figuring out what to do next.

She had the money she'd packed earlier that morning. It would get her a room for the night and some food.

She'd figure out the rest after she got a little sleep.

Noise whispered in the woods ahead, hard to distinguish at first. In her haste to put more distance between herself and Rick, she pushed forward anyway, figuring it could be something as innocuous as a raccoon foraging in the woods ahead.

It was when the noise died into swollen silence that she faltered to a stop, the hair on the back of her neck prickling.

The quiet was tangible, as if some great beast sat just beyond the tree line ahead, holding its breath.

Instinct propelled her backward, first a couple of tentative baby steps to the rear, then a complete about-face. She started running back the way she came, daring only a quick glance behind her to see if she was being followed.

What she saw there made her pounding heart skip a beat.

A dozen men clad in black from their boots to their ski mask–covered faces were gliding through the woods in fast pursuit.

Chapter Five

The woods ahead exploded into noise and activity, sending Rick diving behind the largest piece of cover he could find, a dense mountain-laurel bush that grew along a clump of weathered gray boulders nearby.

Amanda came into view first, running at a full, coltish gallop despite the duffel bag strapped to her back. She almost made it to his position before he saw what she was running from at such a frantic dash.

Several black-clad men with semiautomatic rifles poured through the woods behind her, moving like a dark, lethal wave.

He looked around him wildly, hoping for some miraculous way out of the ambush Amanda had somehow walked right into. The only answer that came his way was a dark notch in the side of the bald mountain face nearby. If he was right—God, how he prayed he was right—there might be a cave carved into that mottled gray stone.

Amanda zigzagged toward him, putting a clump of young pines between her and her pursuers. Rick saw the men in black zigzag right behind her, disappearing momentarily out of sight, blocked by the trees.

It was the best chance he'd have to make his move.

He reached out and grabbed Amanda as she darted past, stifling her soft cry with his palm over her mouth. "Come with me," he growled in her ear, dragging her with him toward the dark spot he prayed would turn out to be a cave.

He could hear the pursuers coming, but they remained out of sight long enough for them to reach the notch in the rock. It was a cave, he saw with shaky relief, small and cramped at the entrance but hollowing out to a larger chamber. He pulled the duffel back off her back and gave her a push through the narrow gap. He tossed the bag inside and followed.

Inside, there was only blackness, save for the sliver of light seeping in from the narrow cave opening. "Not a word," he whispered in her ear, still not letting her go.

Her breathing was fast and harsh to his ears, but he doubted anyone outside the cave would hear them. Still, he stayed completely still and quiet, his ears cocked for any sign that Amanda's pursuers had seen where they'd disappeared to.

He wasn't sure how long they remained motionless. Amanda's breathing softened to a mere whisper, and the rat-a-tat of her heartbeat against his chest slowed to almost normal. He dared a quick glance at his watch and found that they'd been in the cave for at least twenty minutes.

He pulled the small flashlight from his survival kit and flashed it around quickly, getting a quick look at the interior of the cave. It was about twelve feet by twelve feet, with a ceiling rising about ten feet in a dome shape. If necessary, it would be a decent shelter for them for the night.

He just hoped it wouldn't be necessary.

"I'm going to check outside for a minute," he whispered, his lips brushing the curve of her cheek as he bent to speak into her ear.

He felt a little tremble run through her before she responded by clutching him closer, her grip strong. "You called someone, didn't you?" she asked in a voice full of barely contained anger.

"What?" For a moment he thought he'd misunderstood her.

"You called someone while you were out. That's why you really left the room—I told you not to call anyone, so you went out to find a phone." Her hands pushed at his chest, trying to force him away from her.

But he held on to her arms, keeping her close. The last thing he needed was for her to run out of the cave and back into that phalanx of men in black carrying big weapons. "I didn't call anyone." He peered into the gloom, trying to see her face. "Maybe if you'd stayed put like I asked you to—"

"I stayed put for three years, and fat lot of good that did me." She gave another push and broke free of his grasp.

He shot after her as she dashed toward the cave entrance, catching her as she neared the light. "Stop it, Amanda." He didn't dare raise his voice above a whisper, but he infused the soft exhalation with as much force as he could. He could practically smell the panic rising off her skin in waves. He couldn't blame her for losing her grip on her emotions—nothing quite like becoming a killer's target to get the adrenaline pumping in overdrive.

He could see her better, now that they were closer to the fading light seeping through the cave entrance. She looked pale and exhausted, as if the same adrenaline that had kept her on her feet this far had finally sucked her dry of energy.

He couldn't stop himself from cradling her face between his palms. "Stop running. Stay with me."

Her gaze lifted to meet his, her pale eyes wary. "I can't trust you." She looked away. "I can't trust anyone."

His chest ached with sympathy. "Believe me, I know the feeling, baby. But we need each other if we're going to get out of this mess alive."

"They're probably already at the motel, waiting," she growled, pulling away from his touch again. This time, however, she moved away from the cave entrance instead of toward it. "We don't have a chance in hell of getting anywhere near your car."

"I moved the car," he said, smiling slightly as her gaze snapped up to meet his again.

"You thought I'd double back and take it while you were hunting the woods for me?"

She wasn't so tired that her whip-smart mind couldn't cut to the chase, he thought. "The idea crossed my mind."

Her lips flattened with annoyance, but she didn't protest. She could hardly argue with his reasoning, given what had actually transpired. "They could be waiting out there for us right now. Just biding their time."

"I'd like to know how they found us," he said.

"And why there are so many of them," she added, edging toward the cave entrance again.

He caught up with her, keeping his hands to himself for the moment. But if she made a run for it, he'd be ready.

She didn't try to run. She just crept to the edge of the opening and took a quick look outside. She backed up until she bumped into Rick's chest. "I don't see them out there anymore."

"They didn't have a clear line of sight once I pulled you behind the bush," he murmured, enjoying the feel of her small, round backside pressed against his thighs. For a second, he found himself immersed in the memory of that moment they'd shared back in the motel room, when years had seemed to melt into nothing, taking them back to a time where finding pleasure in each other's bodies had seemed as natural as breathing.

He eased away from her before his body betrayed him. "Do you want to take a shot at locating the car? If it's still where I hid it, and they haven't located it, we could get out of here before they found us."

"I'll go. You head for the highway—go to the hamburger place where you got dinner. I'll find the car and come get you." She held out her hand. "Keys?"

He couldn't hold back a soft chuckle. "Not on your life."

One eyebrow arched. "You don't trust me?"

"You haven't exactly given me any reason to."

"I could say the same of you," she pointed out. "You call me and within hours, I'm getting shot at and chased away from my own home—"

"Funny—I'm the only one who actually took a bullet."

She made a small sound of frustration. "So we go together, then. Probably smarter that way."

"Together," he agreed. He looked at the cave entrance. "I'm going to scout out there first, make sure the coast is clear. The last thing we want to do is walk into an ambush."

She looked as if she wanted to protest, but she finally gave a nod. "Okay. Hurry."

Outside, night had already begun to fall, casting the evening sky in deep shades of crimson and purple. It was almost 6:00 p.m., he saw with a quick glance at his watch. He edged toward the mountain-laurel bush where he'd hidden before, stopping at the sound of a faint snapping noise ahead.

Crouching behind the bush, he waited.

There. Movement about fifty yards ahead through the trees and underbrush. In the twilight, the man in black almost blended in with the woods.

Almost.

Moving at a snail's pace, Rick edged backward toward the cave entrance, keeping his eye out for more men in black. He finally reached the narrow slit in the rock and hurried back inside. "There's at least one of them still out there," he whispered to Amanda.

He heard her soft exhalation. "Damn it."

"We could be in worse shape," he pointed out. "You've got water in your pack. Probably more food. We have extra clothes if the temps drop overnight. A roof over our heads."

"So we're staying in this cave tonight?" She sounded so defeated, he thought. Pushed to her limit.

"Can't be much worse than the motel room," he pointed out, deliberately keeping his voice light.

Her gaze slanted his way, and in the faint light from outside, he saw her lips curve. "I'll give you that," she answered, sounding stronger.

"Let's figure out what supplies we have," he suggested. "Ration it out so we have some food and water left over for tomorrow if we have to stay here beyond the night."

With a nod, she picked up the duffel bag and backed deeper into the cave. Finding a place to sit, she unzipped the bag and started digging inside.

"Four twelve-ounce bottles of water," she whispered as he sat down across from her. "Six protein bars."

"Okay—that's one bottle apiece for tonight and one bottle tomorrow. We had protein bars earlier, so we'll save those for tomorrow. Two a day—that'll get us through tomorrow and into the next day."

"I have one of your boxes of ammo."

"I know. I have another box, and if we can get to the car without incident, I have more packed in the trunk."

"What if they find your car?"

It was a possibility, he had to concede. The Charger was hidden from sight on the road, and he'd covered it with some loose limbs he'd foraged from the woods around where he'd parked. But if someone was out there scouring the woods for Amanda, it wouldn't be hard to find the Charger in its hiding place. "We'll deal with that if it arises."

"Are you sure there isn't a tracker of some sort on your car?" she asked a few minutes later.

"Short of tearing it down and putting it back together, I can't be sure," he admitted. "But I looked at all the obvious places, and a few not so obvious ones. I didn't see a thing. And the GPS signal detector I used didn't spot anything."

"If we get out of here, we should check again." She barely got the sentence out past an enormous yawn.

"Why don't you try to get some sleep?" Rick suggested. "You've got to be beat."

Though the light was nearly gone from the cave, he could see her just well enough to notice her back straightening as she spoke. "I'm fine."

She wasn't fine, but if she needed to maintain that facade in front of him, he wasn't going to take that away from her. "Okay. Not going to be much else we can do in here, though. No candles, no books."

"You can sleep if you want to," she said, her tone indifferent.

He wasn't sure he bought the nonchalance, however. There was a faint thread of tension in her voice that made him wonder if she was hiding something from him.

Of course, the more obvious question at this point was, what *wasn't* she hiding from him?

THE NIGHT SEEMED ENDLESS, and despite her determination not to, Amanda fell asleep sometime deep in the morning hours. Following her into her slumber, bleak memories chased her through her dreams, a jumble of horrors and regrets that had been her constant, unwelcome companions almost every night for the past three years.

The dreams always began with no sign of threat in sight. In this dream, she was ten years old again, sitting on the front stoop of the house in McComb, sketching pictures of dragons and unicorns in colored pencils in the sketch pad her Aunt Debbie gave her for her birthday a few days earlier.

She wasn't unaccustomed to the sounds of voices raised in anger. Her mother drank too much, and she tended to pick men who were cruel-mouthed bullies. How much those unpleasant attributes fed on each other was something Amanda had never really been able to decide.

By the age of ten, she'd grown to ignore the fights for the most part, so when the shouts rose over the sounds of birds chirping in the trees and the lawn mower buzzing busily in the neighbor's yard down the street, Amanda blocked out the noise and concentrated on achieving the perfect shimmery green required for a dragon's wing.

The gunshot, however, had ripped through her self-protective cocoon, setting her nerves rattling.

She'd learned not to be afraid of the fights, because none of her mother's boyfriends ever struck blows or made threats. The words that passed between them could be violently ugly, but there were lines they never crossed.

But not that morning.

Slowly, her ten-year-old self turned toward the open screen door and peered through the mesh, telling herself that her mother's boyfriend, Jerry, had turned on the television. That's all it was. He'd turned on the TV to watch one of his favorite cop shows. She listened hard for the sound of voices coming from the set in the kitchen. But all she heard was a low, keening noise that sounded as if hell itself had opened a window to let a song of suffering escape.

She made herself go into the kitchen. Made herself look at the mess her mother had made. Jerry was on the floor, still alive, feebly swinging at her mother with a butcher's knife even as his life blood poured out onto the grimy linoleum—

Amanda woke with a start, that sound still ringing in her

ears. All around her was darkness and cold. Beneath her aching side, the ground was hard stone.

She was in a cave, she remembered. She was decades older than the ten-year-old in her dream, and in the intervening years, she'd seen worse than the scene she'd walked in on that morning in the kitchen of her mother's home.

Much worse.

She felt movement next to her, and her heart skipped a beat. Then she remembered more about where she was and why she was there. Rick Cooper lay on the cold ground beside her, his large, hard-muscled body radiating heat like a furnace. She felt a powerful urge to scoot closer to him, to bask in his warmth. She held herself in check, however, remembering how easily she'd fallen into his arms at the motel the previous day.

Some mistakes didn't need to be repeated, however tempting they might be.

Rick shifted next to her, making a low groaning sound deep in his throat. His breathing, harsh and rapid, didn't sound like normal sleep respiration.

It sounded like a man having a nightmare.

A flutter of sympathy dancing in her chest, she reached to her side and found the small survival kit she'd taken from Rick's bag before she fled the motel. She took the compact flashlight from inside and snapped it on, letting the narrow beam glance across Rick's face.

His eyes were still closed, but there was nothing peaceful about his expression. Deep furrows creased his forehead and the skin around his eyes, making him look ages older than his thirty-five years. Despite the cold, sweat beads had formed on his brow, glittering in the flashlight beam.

Was he ill?

Edging closer, she laid the back of her hand against his

forehead and found him warm but not feverish. Releasing a soft sigh of relief, she started to sit back.

Like a striking snake, Rick reached out and grabbed her hand, his eyes snapping open.

For a second, even though she knew she was strong enough and well-trained enough to hold her own in a fight, Amanda felt a flicker of fear. Because the cold light in Rick's dark eyes was nothing short of lethal.

"It's me," she whispered, not because she was trying to be quiet but because her voice failed her.

His expression softened, though he didn't let go of her wrist. "Turn off the light," he commanded softly, sitting up.

Her finger trembled on the switch, unwilling to extinguish the only thing keeping this cave from once again becoming a cold, black void.

"Amanda?" His voice remained quiet but with a harsh edge that made her stomach knot. "The light."

She forced herself to push the button, plunging them into inky nothingness. For a second, she thought she felt icy fingers crawling down her spine, trailing goose bumps. She felt the immediate jump in her pulse and tried to slow her breathing to compensate. But the only thing she succeeded in doing was making herself feel light-headed.

"Rick?" she whispered, not because she had anything to say but just to reassure herself he was still there.

"I'm here," he answered, his voice little more than a breath in the dark.

She reached for him, her fingers colliding with the rock wall of his chest. She felt his heartbeat quicken beneath her touch, and for a moment, the urge to curl herself around him was almost more than she could resist.

"How's your arm?" she asked.

"Hurts like an SOB. But I think I'll live."

"I could put some more ointment on it." Anything to take her mind off the gaping maw of blackness.

"You can't see it in the dark." Humor tinted his low murmur. "I don't think I want to risk you poking me right in the wound."

His voice was so familiar, even after almost three years apart. Of course, she'd held on to his voice, trapped it in her mind during the worst of those days in Kaziristan, when the icy night winds rattled the eaves of the mud house where they'd kept her prisoner.

For the first days, she'd been kept utterly in the dark. Al Adar's version of sensory deprivation, she supposed. For the first couple of days, she'd even kept her spirits up. They hadn't raped her, and she considered that fact a good sign that she'd be able to get through the ordeal without coming apart.

But that had been before she realized just how many ways there were to rape a person that had nothing to do with sex.

After the first session with a man she'd known only as Raa Baber—The Tiger—she'd conjured up Rick's soft voice, bathing her wounds in the remembered sound of his faint Southern drawl.

He'd told her, just yesterday, that living back in the South had reanimated her Mississippi accent. His was stronger now, too, richer and more fully formed, as if he'd rediscovered a missing piece of himself when he left MacLear behind.

"How long have you been back home in Alabama?" she asked.

There was a long pause, as if the question caught him by surprise. She had the strange sensation that he was staring right at her, even though there was no way he could see her in the dark.

"A little over a year," he answered. She heard his body

shift in the void beside her, as if he'd stretched back out on the hard cave floor. Tempted to curl up next to him and let his heat drive away her bone-deep chill, she dug her fingertips into her palm and turned her gaze in a different direction.

Though she expected to see no variation in the unrelenting gloom, she spotted a faint lightening a few feet away, diluting the dark. The cave entrance, she realized. Moonlight must be drifting in from outside. She felt the tug of that soft whisper of light as if it were a living thing.

"Maybe I should check to see if someone's outside." She sat up on her knees, preparing to stand.

"Where are you going?" He caught her arm, holding her in place. She bit back a soft gasp as his fingers tightened on a sore place on her arm. Had she injured herself during her mad dash through the woods?

His fingers loosened and fell away. "Did I hurt you?"

"No," she said, but the burning in her arm hadn't subsided. She lifted her fingers, pressing the sore area. She felt a rip in her jacket and a sticky wetness. "I think I cut myself—"

She heard a rustling noise, then a snick. Light cut through the gloom, making her squint.

"Let me see." Rick pointed his flashlight at her arm.

Looking down, she saw a ragged furrow in the arm of her olive-drab jacket, just above the elbow. The edges were singed and damp with drying blood. She knew exactly what it was, even before Rick spoke.

"They shot you," he said in a strangled voice.

Chapter Six

Amanda stared at the groove in her flesh, feeling a little queasy. She forced steel into her spine and lifted her chin to meet Rick's worried gaze. "Must have grazed me—I don't remember feeling anything." Of course, she'd been hauling butt through the woods at the time—any number of branches and limbs had caught her clothing and skin as she ran, leaving plenty of scratches and bruises.

"I didn't hear any gunshots from where I was," Rick remarked.

She also didn't remember hearing a gunshot, but she'd been running at full tilt, her pulse thundering in her ears. "Sound suppressors?" she suggested. She might not have heard the flat, muffled blat of suppressed gunfire in the chaos.

"If they're former MacLear Special Services Unit agents, I wouldn't be surprised," he admitted, turning the flashlight to the ground, searching for something. "The SSU didn't exactly want stories about what they were doing to get around."

She watched the faint beam settle on her duffel bag. "What did they do, exactly?"

"Well, the rest of us didn't know the SSU existed until everything blew up a little over a year ago." Rick opened her duffel bag and withdrew the first-aid kit she'd packed inside. *His* first-aid kit, she thought with a touch of embarrassment. The arched-eyebrow look he gave her only exacerbated her sense of guilt. But he said nothing.

"What happened a year ago?" She pulled off her jacket and rolled up her sleeve to get a better look at the wound. Without the flashlight beam pointed directly at her arm, all she could make out in the shadows was a thin, dark furrow in the flesh above her elbow. At his look of surprise, she added, "I don't watch a lot of news. I knew MacLear had folded, but I never heard exactly why."

"Barton Reid sent a group of the SSU to kidnap the two-year-old son of a linguist named Abby Chandler."

She looked at him, puzzled. "A linguist?"

"They wanted something her late husband had stolen from MacLear."

When Rick flashed the light on her arm, she winced at the ragged, oozing sight. She should have checked before they settled down for the night—her arm had been aching a little then. She just hadn't wanted to admit any weakness in front of Rick. "What time is it?"

"A little after 4:00 a.m."

So the wound had been dirty for several hours now. "Better give it a good scrubbing," she said grimly. "Infection's had some time to set in."

With a look of sympathy, Rick nodded and went to work on the wound with methodical thoroughness. He was trying to be gentle, Amanda could tell, but there was no painless way to scrub dirt and debris out of an open wound, especially one that had been allowed to fester all night.

He spoke while he worked, his voice soft but somehow bracing. "Abby—the linguist—didn't know what her husband had taken or where to find it, so she went to her husband's best friend, a fellow Marine named Luke Cooper."

She looked up at the name. "Cooper?" she asked in a similarly hushed tone.

He nodded. "My cousin."

"Ah."

"Abby figured if anyone would know what her husband had taken, it would be Luke."

"And did he know?"

"Not at first." To her great relief, Rick stopped cleaning the wound and reached into the first-aid kit for the same tube of ointment she'd used to protect his earlier gunshot wound. His mind seemed to follow a similar path, for he smiled slightly as he started applying the ointment. "Look—matching wounds."

"I take it, since MacLear went down in a blaze of infamy, that your cousin found what the linguist was looking for?"

"Yeah. And a lot more." Rick put a piece of gauze bandaging over her bullet graze. "Found out her little boy was actually his son. It's a long story, but one with a happy ending. He and Abby are married now."

"And they put Barton Reid behind bars?" She'd had some dealings with Reid during her time in the CIA. Not good dealings—the man had been the worst kind of diplomat, one who thought his position in the State Department gave him a sort of *droit du seigneur*—not sexually, as far as she knew, but Reid had expected everyone else, fellow American and host-country citizen alike, to march to his tune. He'd been the kind of foreign-service agent who gave the rest of them a bad name, and she wasn't sorry to hear that he'd been hoist with his own petard. "What did he do?"

"Profited from a drugs-for-arms deal down in Sanselmo."

"And whatever Abby's husband stole proved it?"

"Well, we thought so, at the time." He sounded grim. "There were copies of emails, saved on a flash drive, that showed Reid had direct knowledge of the deals."

"But?"

"But Reid claims the mails were sent fraudulently by one

of his aides. A man who conveniently committed suicide a week before Reid came out with this claim."

Amanda shook her head. "Surely nobody's fooled by that."

He shot her an odd look. "You haven't heard *any* of this before? Thurlow Gap didn't have a newspaper?"

"I didn't take the paper," she answered.

"It's been all over the news for the past few months."

"I told you, I don't watch the news," she replied, her tone louder than she had intended. She lowered her voice back to a whisper. "I was trying to leave all of that behind me."

She could tell he wanted to ask more questions, but to her relief, he simply finished taping down her bandage and sat back on his heels. "It'll be getting light out soon," he said. "Maybe this *would* be a good time to see if our intruders have finally left."

Amanda felt sluggish as she grabbed her gun from its position beside her and struggled to her feet behind him, catching up only when he slowed at the cave entrance. Morning light filtering through the trees outside bounced off the pale gray face of the cave entrance, providing just enough illumination for her to see the tension in Rick's face.

"Stay," he said, although almost no sound escaped his lips. "I'll be right back."

She wanted to protest, but her whole brain seemed cloudy, as if she hadn't yet shaken off the effects of sleep. She checked the clip of her Smith & Wesson as quietly as she could and pressed her back against the cave wall, waiting for some sort of signal from Rick.

He reappeared in the cave entrance. "It's clear," he said aloud, his voice sounding thunderous after such a long period of hushed tones. "At least, right around here."

"Do you know how to get out of here?"

"I know the general direction. But we can't go back the

way you came—you left a trail. They had plenty of time to follow it back to the motel. They probably have someone waiting there for us if we go back."

Her stomach turned an unpleasant flip. "What if they've found your car?"

"We'll find out soon enough."

They headed out into the gray premorning gloom, although even the little bit of light inching its way into the eastern sky was bright after a night in the rocky bowels of the mountainside. Rick consulted the compass in his survival pack and headed them toward the rising sun. He seemed to know where he was going, and she was feeling too exhausted to argue. Nor did she put up a fight when he picked up her duffel bag and slung it over his shoulder.

They seemed to trudge through the woods forever, although when she asked Rick for the time, she was surprised to learn they'd been walking for less than twenty minutes. Her legs felt weak and achy, and her head was starting to hurt. He offered her a protein bar when they stopped for a second to regain their bearings, but she refused it. Her brain told her she needed the fuel, but her squirming gut warned that it had no intention of accepting food at the moment.

She did take a sip from the water bottle in her own pack. The water felt cold and delicious, and she had to force herself not to drink the whole bottle in one swig.

About ten minutes later, she heard the faint sound of traffic. The road must be somewhere nearby.

"There," Rick said quietly.

She followed his gaze and saw a clump of bushes about twenty feet from a pale gray ribbon of county highway. "What?"

"See that clump of elderberry bushes?"

She wasn't sure what an elderberry bush looked like, but she guessed he was talking about the clump ahead. "Yeah?"

"That's the Charger."

She peered at the bushes. If the big black Dodge was parked under there, it wasn't readily obvious. Of course, there was barely any daylight at all. Perhaps it would be more visible once the sun came up.

"Still have that GPS signal detector on you?" she asked.

"Yeah." He pulled it from the survival pack attached to his belt and turned it on. A bright light came on immediately.

Her gut tightened. "That's a hit, isn't it?"

He nodded, his forehead furrowed. "But it's not coming from the car."

"What do you mean?"

"This device can detect a signal within a twenty-five-foot radius. We're at least fifty feet from the car."

"One of us? When would anyone have had a chance to put a tracker on one of us?"

"Wait here." He walked toward the car, stepping out his paces. About thirty feet away, he turned, looking back at her. Slowly, he walked back. "It's not me. The light went off about twenty-five feet out."

She held out her hand for the device, her heart sinking. Stripping off the survival kit and handing Rick her pistol, so that all she carried with her was her clothing on her back, she slowly paced off. Ten feet. Twenty. Ten more, and she stood about thirty feet away from both Rick and the Charger.

The light was still shining brightly.

She looked at Rick, who was watching her with a mixture of curiosity and alarm. "It's on me," she said.

"Did you miss something in your pockets?" he asked.

She checked the pocket of her jeans. Nothing. Her T-shirt didn't have any pockets. Carefully, she reached down and pulled off her sturdy hiking boots. She threw them underhand to Rick and checked the GPS signal detector. Still shining brightly.

"Could it be in the button of your jeans?" Rick asked.

She shimmied out of her jeans, rolled them into a ball and threw them toward Rick. They landed within the twenty-five-foot zone, but after he'd retrieved them and carried them back to the safe zone, the light was still shining.

"What if it's not in your clothes?" Rick said, his tone so hushed that she could barely make out what he was saying.

The nausea she'd been battling for the past half hour rose to a crescendo as a horrible new thought flashed in her mind.

What if the tracking chip were inside her?

It would explain how Alexander Quinn had known where to send his cryptic message. How their pursuers had tracked them on the highway and later to where she'd hiked through the woods. "They've been tracking me this whole time."

Rick crossed to her, bringing her discarded items. Shivering from the cold and from reaction setting in, she tugged on her jeans and pulled on her boots.

Rick wrapped her jacket around her and pulled her into the curve of his arm. "If it's on you, we can't hang around here much longer. They may already have your signal back."

"The cave could have blocked the signal last night," she murmured, trying to work past the acute sense of violation.

"Have you had surgery anytime recently?" he asked.

She shook her head. The injuries from her captivity in Kaziristan had been painful and debilitating, but they hadn't required surgery. She hadn't even gone under anesthesia afterward—the closest she'd come was a shot of Novocain at the CIA dentist's office when they capped the molar her tormenters had broken during a torture session.

"Son of a—" She pressed her fingertips against her jaw.

"What is it?"

She grabbed her duffel bag from the ground by his side

and pulled a small tool kit from inside. The set of pliers inside should do what she needed.

"What the hell are you doing?" Rick asked as she opened her mouth and clamped the pliers over the crowned molar.

She gave a couple of hard tugs and the crown came free. She dropped it in her palm and studied the underside of the fake porcelain tooth.

There it was, embedded in the underside of the crown. The chip was tiny—about an eighth of an inch square—but incredibly complex-looking.

Rick's dark eyes met hers, his expression tinged with horror. "Someone put a tracker in your crown?"

She nodded, swallowing another surge of nausea. "Let's get rid of it and get out of here." She started to throw the crown into the woods.

"Wait—" Rick caught her hand, stopping her. "How was the signal getting through the porcelain?"

He plucked the crown from her hand and studied the chip inside. "Let me borrow those pliers." Using the tool, he carefully picked out the small chip. "There it is."

She bent closer to look where he was pointing with the tip of the pliers. A tiny wire, attached to the chip, stuck out of the porcelain.

Rick turned the crown over and pointed to a small spot at the top of the false tooth. "That's an antenna—it's threaded through the porcelain. It would have sent out a signal, possibly through the skin of your cheek, but definitely anytime you opened your mouth." He handed the tooth back to her, keeping the chip. "When we get to Chickasaw County, we'll find a dental-repair kit and put that back on for you. Without the chip, it's harmless."

When we get to Chickasaw County, she repeated silently. He still expected her to go home with him, after everything they'd just been through. Did he really think people bold and ruthless enough to send a whole crew of assassins after her would stop looking for her just because they lost her signal?

"What are you going to do with that?" She nodded toward the chip, which he was examining with curiosity.

His gaze shifted toward the road, where traffic had begun to pick up a bit. A couple of cars passed by while she waited for his answer.

"Take this. I'm going to flag someone down. If I can get a vehicle to stop, I want you to slip this chip into their back bumper while I talk to the driver." He touched her face, his hands impossibly warm on her cold cheeks. "You up to it?"

She lifted her chin, fighting a sense of enervation. "Let's do it."

She followed him to the road's edge, her leg muscles aching and trembling as if she'd run a marathon. The first couple of cars passed without stopping, but finally a dusty old pickup truck slowed and pulled onto the shoulder. The window rolled down and a tanned, grizzled farmer wearing a blue plaid shirt and denim overalls stuck his head out the window. "You folks in some kind of trouble?"

"We went hiking yesterday and got lost," Rick told the man. As he spun a tale of a vacation gone wrong, Amanda edged back to the truck's bumper and dropped the chip into the truck bed, where it quickly joined the road grit lining the grimy bed.

"Well, the motel is down the road that way—you can't miss it," the farmer told them. "Need a ride? Your missus looks a little tuckered out."

Rick put his arm around Amanda's shoulder. "No, I can get her there okay. But thanks for the offer." He waved as the farmer drove away.

"Let's go—just in case they've already tracked us this far," Rick said, heading for the car.

"What if we've just put that man in danger?" Amanda asked as she trudged through the underbrush after him.

He turned to look at her. "I didn't even think of that."

"I didn't until it was too late," she admitted. But she should have. She'd spent a lot of time over the past three years worrying about collateral damage—had she put her neighbors in Thurlow Gap in danger just by living among them?

"My guess is, he'll be okay. They didn't come after me in the motel—they went after you. They know exactly who they're looking for, and they're not going to make a big scene and draw attention by ambushing some poor farmer in a pickup truck who's just going on with his daily business."

Amanda hoped he was right. But she couldn't help worrying about the farmer.

Or whoever Rick was talking to on his cell phone when she woke from a light doze almost an hour later in time to overhear him say, "We're about twenty minutes away from your location. Thanks for the escort in."

"Twenty minutes from where?" Amanda asked, her voice thick with sleep.

"Fort Payne, Alabama," he answered, ending the call. "That was my sister Isabel. She and my brother Wade are meeting us there to give us a security escort to Chickasaw County."

She shook her head, wincing as the movement intensified the pain savaging her skull. "Don't involve anyone else—I should just..." The world outside the car seemed to be moving in a dizzying rush, the blur of colors making her light-headed.

"Amanda?" Rick's voice, heavy with alarm, seemed to come from miles away.

She closed her eyes against the kaleidoscope of images

assaulting her throbbing brain. If she could just shut it out for a little while…

Blackness descended, and for the first time in a long time, she sank gratefully into the abyss.

SHE WAS BURNING UP, so feverish that her flesh almost seemed to sting his fingers where he touched her. On a hunch, he tugged up the sleeve of her jacket and saw that the skin outside the bandage over her bullet graze was turning a purplish-red from infection.

She'd gone too long without cleaning the wound. Longer than he had, and he'd been careful to protect his own injury from contamination, keeping it covered by his shirt.

There was a temporal thermometer in the first-aid kit. At the first opportunity, he pulled off to the side of the road and tested her temperature, trying not to wake her. She was asleep, not unconscious—she'd roused and grumbled a little earlier when he'd felt her forehead—and he knew that rest was almost as good a remedy for infection as antibiotics.

He checked the thermometer when it beeped. Her temperature was nearly 104 degrees. Too high.

The small scenic overlook where he'd parked to take her temperature was empty of other cars. Not that having an audience would have stopped him from what he was about to do, but he knew Amanda would probably prefer not to be stripped naked with people watching.

He went around to her side of the car, carrying a couple of ibuprofen, a bottle of water and a clean washcloth he kept in his larger camping kit packed in the trunk of the car. First coaxing her to take the ibuprofen with a few sips of the water, he then turned his attention to bringing her fever down. He planned to strip her to her underwear and bathe her with the wet washcloth. The cool water and the mild

March morning temperatures should be the next best thing to an ice bath.

But Amanda's fierce reaction when he started to remove her T-shirt caught him by surprise. She swung at him weakly as he pulled the hem up to her breastbone. "No!" she cried, slapping at his hands.

But he didn't drop the hem, his gaze snared by what he saw along the edge of her rib cage. Fending off her struggle, he turned her until her back was bared to him from the shoulder blades down.

Still-healing red scars crisscrossed her back like a roadmap of hell. Rick had seen scars like that before, in any number of war-torn snake pits and soul-rending refugee camps.

Whip scars. A sign that she'd been beaten, at the very least. But beatings almost always came with other kinds of torture in places like Kaziristan.

He let the T-shirt drop and laid his hand on her face, soothing her back to a calm slumber, while inside, his heart felt as if it had been shredded and left to bleed.

"Oh, baby," he whispered, pressing his lips to her hot forehead, "who did this to you?"

Chapter Seven

"So this is her." The voice was low-pitched and female, with a hint of a Southern accent.

"She's going by Amanda Caldwell," Rick's voice answered the female voice. "She doesn't want to be called Tara."

He sounded sad, Amanda thought. Sad that she didn't want him to call her Tara anymore? Or was his sadness a sign of something worse?

Was she dying? She felt as if she were dying, the way her head pounded as if someone were drilling a jackhammer into the top of her skull. And where she'd been so cold just a little while ago, now she was flushed and sweaty, her T-shirt clammy against her skin.

She tried opening her eyes and regretted it. Light assaulted her pupils, making them contract painfully. She squeezed her eyes shut.

"She's awake." That voice was all male and as Southern as turnip greens, delivering the news of her awakening in a flat, just-the-facts tone.

Amanda forced her eyes open again. The light didn't seem as painful this time. Her vision was a little blurry, but when Rick's familiar face came into view, her eyes focused enough to see his look of relief.

"Hey there," he said quietly, sitting next to her. She was in a bed, she realized. Not a hospital bed—the mattress under her was soft and comfortable. As home should be.

She was in a bedroom, large and casually pretty, with walls painted a soothing eggshell-blue and plain brown curtains flanking the tall windows. She tried to sit up but stopped immediately as a wave of nausea pulsed through her gut.

"I need a trash can," she moaned.

"Here." The owner of the female voice thrust a small garbage can, lined with plastic, into Amanda's hands. Just before her stomach rebelled, Amanda caught a glimpse of the woman who went with the voice, a tall, striking woman with curly dark hair and sympathetic eyes the color of strong tea.

There was nothing left in her stomach, so she had to wait through a series of dry heaves before she could finally sit back, moaning, and wait for the gnawing pain in her gut to subside. She looked up at Rick, mortified. "I'm sorry."

It was the woman who answered her, tugging Rick out of his position beside the bed. She sat in the place he'd vacated, offering a wet washcloth to her. "No apology necessary. You've been running a high fever for the past couple of hours. Rick says you haven't eaten since sometime yesterday?"

The thought of food made her stomach cramp, but she nodded.

"You want to try a little beef broth?"

Amanda started to shake her head no, then realized that her nausea might be exacerbated by hunger. So she changed the gesture to a nod.

"Rick, there's a can in the cabinet. Go heat it up." Isabel flashed him a wry smile. "Oh—and empty that trash can for me, will you? Wade," she added, turning to the other person, a dark-haired man a couple of inches shorter than Rick, "you head back to the office and let everyone there know what's going on. And grab Eric—I think she needs him to take a look at her."

Both men headed out of the room—Wade walking with a distinct limp, Amanda noticed—leaving Amanda alone with the woman, who watched her with gentle eyes.

"You must be Isabel," Amanda rasped, her throat sore from the dry heaves.

"Yes. I'm Rick's sister. And the other guy was our brother Wade." She patted Amanda's leg. "You feeling any better? You still look pretty pale."

"Has my fever broken?"

Isabel touched Amanda's forehead with the back of her hand. "You feel cooler. And you're sweating now—that's a good sign."

"Who's Eric?" Amanda asked, remembering what Isabel had said to her brother Wade.

"He works with us at Cooper Security. Used to be a Navy medical officer, then he joined our agency. Sort of our private physician. Plus he's our go-to guy on medical-related investigations. He'll assess your condition and tell us whether you need to go to the hospital."

Amanda shook her head, ignoring the resulting pain. "No hospital."

"Look, I get that you don't want to be found. From what Rick tells us, I understand completely. But letting yourself die of an infection doesn't solve anything."

"I've had worse wounds," Amanda answered flatly.

Isabel's eyes softened even more. "We saw the scars."

Amanda's heart sank. "Rick saw them?"

Isabel nodded. "You don't get scars like that unless you've been tortured."

Amanda pressed her lips into a tight line, aching with humiliation. "It's over. I survived."

"Where did it happen?"

She shot Rick's sister a warning look.

Isabel sat back, her expression shifting to neutral. "Okay. We'll get you back on your feet again and then you can decide what you want to do next. Sound like a plan?"

Amanda didn't want to like Isabel Cooper, but she found the woman's matter-of-fact approach and calm demeanor soothing. She didn't want to be coddled or treated like a victim, and Isabel seemed to get that.

It made Amanda all the more curious about the thread of sadness she saw in Isabel's dark gaze. Maybe she was battling a few demons of her own.

"Where am I?" she asked.

"My house." Isabel looked around the room, a faint smile of affection curving her mouth. "It's really too big for one person, but it was so homey and comfortable. And it's about ten minutes from the office and just down the street from where my dad lives. I couldn't pass it up."

"Last I knew, you were in the FBI," Amanda commented. "At least, that's what Rick said." She couldn't really be sure how much of what he'd told her in Kaziristan was the truth. In a lot of ways, he'd been as much a secret-keeper as she'd been.

"I was." Isabel's tone held a touch of bleakness, and Amanda realized she'd stumbled onto a clue to the sadness she'd seen in the woman's eyes. But she was in no position to ask any questions, given how she'd blocked Isabel's attempts to learn more about her own scars.

"So you quit to work for your brother?"

Isabel's tone returned to normal. "Yes. About five months ago. I needed a change, and Jesse's trying to build Cooper Security into a top-notch agency."

"I guess grabbing an FBI agent away from the bureau might be quite a coup," Amanda ventured.

Isabel laughed. "We're like a big ol' bowl of alphabet soup," she answered, her Alabama accent stronger than before. "Former FBI, DEA, DSS, ATF—and Wade swears one of the former Special Forces guys we hired was really working for the CIA in Afghanistan." She lowered her voice, her eyes glittering with humor. "But if Mac told us the truth, he'd have to kill us."

Rick came back into the room, stopping in the doorway as if to make sure it was all right to enter. Amanda met his gaze, wondering if she'd see pity there, now that he'd seen her scars.

She didn't know if she could bear his pity.

But his expression, while sympathetic, also seemed tinged with admiration, as if he were more focused on her survival than the ordeal itself. She wanted it to stay that way. It's how she managed to deal with life these days, herself—by concentrating on how far she'd come from the trembling, broken creature who'd managed to break out of her prison and struggle to freedom only moments before, she was convinced, she'd have sunk into irretrievable madness.

"I made some toast, in case you want something a little more solid than broth." He carried a flat bamboo tray to the bedside and set it on the table at her elbow. "You look a little brighter-eyed."

"I feel a little better," she admitted. It was true—the pain in her head had settled into a nagging ache instead of crushing agony, and the smell of hot broth and freshly toasted bread was kick-starting the appetite she had believed, moments earlier, she'd never discover again.

"Wade says Eric's on his way," Rick said to Isabel, then looked at Amanda. "He's a former Navy medical officer—"

"I told her." Isabel touched her brother's arm. "He needs to look at your wound, too." She looked at Amanda. "Don't let him play tough guy and forget to tell Eric about his injury."

"I won't."

Isabel left the room, closing the door behind her.

Rick picked up the tray. "You ready for this?"

Amanda pushed herself into a more upright position. To her relief, neither the jackhammer in her head nor the twisting nausea returned with the movement. She held out her hands for the tray and tried a few sips of the broth.

Within a few minutes, she'd finished the whole bowl as well as the piece of toast. She'd been afraid the food in her stomach would only make her feel sicker, but the opposite happened instead. Her queasiness eased away to nothing, and even her headache had dulled another few notches.

"Now that's more like the woman I know and..." Rick stopped short, smiling a little self-consciously. "You were pretty out of it for a while there."

"Sorry about that."

"I was worried you were unconscious, but you fought me well enough when I tried to give you a sponge bath."

That must have been when he'd seen her scars. She tried not to cringe at the thought. "Strange," she said lightly. "A sponge bath sounds like a lovely idea. A bubble bath would be even better."

He arched an eyebrow. "You always did love your creature comforts."

She laughed softly at how he must remember her from their brief days together. Her CIA cover had been embassy liaison with an American natural gas company in Kaziristan, and she'd played the part to the hilt, wearing designer suits and five-hundred-dollar shoes, eating only in the handful of haute cuisine restaurants to be found in Tablis, the once urbane but rapidly deteriorating capital city of Kaziristan. "You know most of that was part of the cover story, right?"

"I knew," he said with a slight smile. "When we were alone, you let more of who you really are show than you probably think. I mean, you kicked off those four-inch stiletto heels the second you got in the door of your flat, and changed clothes immediately."

A rush of heat accompanied a sudden flash of memory—Rick had removed her clothes himself, more often than not. They'd had so little time to be alone with each other, in those tumultuous days before Tablis exploded into the violence that the nation was still struggling to recover from. Every chance they got they'd spent exploring each other, as if kisses and caresses could overcome the secrets they'd had to keep from one another.

It had seemed so real at the time, the passion and devotion developing between them. To this day, she couldn't remember those weeks with Rick without aching to relive those stolen moments. Maybe she'd believed the promises they'd made, not with words but with passion-darkened gazes and sweat-slick bodies straining to become one.

The quick rap on the door jolted through her system like a shock. Rick answered the door, coming back with a tall, handsome man wearing a smile that didn't quite make it all the way to his cool blue eyes. Rick introduced him as Eric Brannon. "Eric, this is Amanda."

"Nice to meet you, Amanda." Eric pulled up a chair beside her and dispensed with further small talk, lifting the edge of her T-shirt sleeve to remove the bandage. The gauze stuck to the dried blood of her wound, making her grimace with pain.

"Sorry about that."

"No problem." She took a quick peek at the bloody groove in her arm and saw, with some surprise, that the infection didn't look nearly as bad as she'd feared. The wound also seemed smaller, in this cozy room, than it had appeared in that dank cave.

"Well, it's infected," Eric said flatly a few minutes later. "But not as badly as it could be."

"She was pretty out of it when we were driving in." Rick gave her a worried look.

"We'd been on the move for nearly twenty-four hours," she pointed out with a wry smile. "I don't know about you, but I'm not as young as I used to be…."

"Exhaustion definitely could have been a contributing factor. And if you hadn't eaten in a while—"

"One protein bar around five o'clock last night. Nothing before or since until just now." They'd thrown away the burgers that had sat overnight in the car while they were dodging the black-clad hunters, and she'd been too sick at that point to want anything for breakfast anyway.

"Well, there you go." Eric opened his bag and withdrew a few supplies, getting right to work cleaning out the infected wound. It hurt like hell, bringing tears to her eyes more than once, but she forced them back, refusing to show weakness in front of either man.

Rick, for his part, winced in sympathy as he watched Eric work. "What about oral antibiotics?" he asked.

"I've got a shot that will get things started, then I'll prescribe oral antibiotics that should knock out the infection in no time." Eric smiled that not-quite-a-smile at Amanda once more, piquing her innate curiosity. Something was bothering the good doctor, and the former CIA agent in her wanted the full story. Just as she was similarly intrigued by the sadness in Isabel Cooper's eyes.

It had been a long time since she'd let herself become concerned with what was going on in the lives of people around her. She wasn't sure the return of her nosy instincts was a good thing—she'd fared quite well for over the past few years by keeping to herself and letting the world around her turn without her.

Eric gave her the shot in her hip and sat back. "That should kick in soon and make you feel a lot better pretty quickly. You should rest as much as you can over the next few days and try not to skip meals."

"Can I take a shower?"

"Yeah—it probably won't hurt to clean that wound again." He looked at Rick. "You can bandage it when she's done?"

"Sure."

The doctor glanced at Rick's left arm, where the bulk of the bandage showed beneath the cotton of his long-sleeve shirt. "I hear you have a wound of your own I need to look at."

With a sigh, Rick shrugged off his shirt, baring not only the bandage she'd applied the day before but his broad shoulders, flat stomach and powerful chest. Whatever else he'd been doing over the past three years, he'd been staying in good shape. He looked as fit and strong as she remembered.

She knew he couldn't say the same for her. She'd lost at least fifteen pounds since her escape from al Adar.

If only that had been all she'd lost.

RICK WALKED ERIC TO THE front door of his sister Isabel's house. "Is she going to be okay?"

"I think so. Infections can always get worse, but we caught it early, and if she follows my instructions, as long as she doesn't have any underlying immune system issues, she should be back to her old self in a few days. The wound will probably leave a scar, but none of the underlying muscle tissue seems to be affected. She should have full use of her arm." Eric slanted an amused look at Rick. "Your arm should be fine, too, tough guy. Looks like you treated it quickly after the injury, which always helps."

In his worry about Amanda, Rick had almost forgotten about his own injured arm. It barely hurt unless he moved it around too much. "Do you have to report our gunshot wounds to the authorities?" He didn't want the cops involved if he could help it. He knew Amanda would balk at the idea.

"I get the feeling mentioning anything to anyone about your friend being here would do more harm than good, right?"

Rick nodded.

Eric smiled. "So, I treated two deep abrasions today."

"First, do no harm?"

"Exactly."

Rick closed the door behind the doctor and returned to Isabel's spare room, half hoping Amanda would already be asleep. He wasn't exactly looking forward to the conversation he and she needed to have.

But Amanda was sitting in the chair by the window, looking out at the sprawling backyard of his sister's house. "Nice view," she murmured. "I miss the Smoky Mountains outside my door, but this is a lovely area, too."

"We're on the mountain," he murmured, squelching the urge to touch her pale cheek. "Our office is in Maybridge, on the northern edge of Gossamer Mountain. Here on the southern side is Gossamer Ridge—most of my family and some of my cousins live there."

She leaned her head up to look at him. "The cousin you were telling me about—the one who got crossways with Barton Reid? Does he live in Gossamer Ridge?"

Rick nodded. "He does now."

"Good." She looked back at the window. "I think I'd like to talk to him."

"I can arrange that," Rick said, crouching beside her. "I think there's something else we need to talk about first."

She turned her head to look at him again, her gaze bleak. "Do we have to?"

"Yeah, we do."

She released a soft sigh but said nothing else.

He asked the question as gently as he could. "Who gave you those scars?"

"Do you remember the day we called it quits?"

"Of course." The memory of her walking away on a Tablis street, spine straight, chin up and her heels clicking on the cobblestones as she disappeared from his life, was an image that still haunted his dreams.

"I turned the corner near the florist shop and headed back toward the embassy. I made it almost to the patisserie." Her voice grew faint, as if she'd disappeared from him again.

He caught her chin in his palm, drawing her face around to look at him. He was afraid of her answer to the next question, because only one answer made sense. And it was a fate he wouldn't wish on his worst enemy. "Who did this to you?"

She said the words he dreaded. "Al Adar."

Chapter Eight

She saw the horror in his eyes and realized that no matter what nightmares she'd had to face for the four and a half weeks she'd spent in al Adar's torture dungeon, it could have been worse. It could have been what he was clearly imagining.

"They didn't rape me," she said quickly, because she knew it would be his first thought. It would have been her first thought, as well, had a colleague been taken by the terrorist group, which had built a reputation for utter, soulless ruthlessness over the five-year period when it tried to destroy the remaining shaky hold of democratic ideals in the Central Asian republic.

She saw the relief in his expression, but it didn't last long. Like anyone who'd spent time living in Kaziristan, Rick knew that there were plenty of atrocities al Adar was known for besides rape.

He caught her hand, looking at her short fingernails. He couldn't miss the differences—when her nails had been torn off during torture sessions, the last thing her captors had cared about was whether or not they'd grow back properly. A couple of the fingernail beds had become infected, and the nails had only recently grown back enough to look halfway normal. Doctors had warned those nails might never be right again.

Compared with the sorts of deformities some surviving al Adar victims had to live with, misshapen nails and a few scars on her torso seemed small nuisances. She knew her fate could have been much worse.

Besides, some of the worst scars of her ordeal remained hidden inside.

She gently pulled her hands out of his grip. “They wanted me to tell them about a man they were looking for. I’m pretty sure they knew I was CIA, so you’d think they’d have asked about state secrets, wouldn’t you?”

“A man?”

“I didn’t even know who he was. But they seemed to think I knew where they could find him.”

She saw Rick’s eyes narrow. “Did they tell you his name?”

“They called him The Doctor. They seemed to think I would know who they meant.”

The odd expression on Rick’s face persisted, but she felt too ill and tired to try to figure out what he was thinking. She hadn’t wanted to talk about her ordeal in Kaziristan in the first place, and right now, the call of the bed behind her was growing strong.

“But you didn’t?”

“No, I didn’t. I tried to pretend I did—so they wouldn’t just kill me before I figured out how to get away from them.”

He reached up and brushed away the lock of tangled hair that had fallen in her face. “Smart lady.”

She smiled a little at his praise, forcing herself to ignore the way even that light touch made her whole body tingle with awareness. “Toward the end, I was beginning to think I was being stupid, instead. Prolonging the ordeal when I could have just gotten it over with.”

“But you got away.”

“I did.” She told him about Malid, the guard she’d targeted the day she'd made her escape attempt. "He had a large scar on the left side of his forehead—I figured he'd had a head injury at some point in his life that left him slightly brain damaged. He spoke Kaziri with a strong rural accent and a thick-tongued speech impediment."

"Go for the weakest link."

She nodded. "I tricked him into loosening my shackles. Once he got close enough, and I had him off guard, I just followed my training." If Malid hadn't been a quick-tempered brute, she might have felt a little sorry for what had surely happened to him after his superiors in the organization discovered he'd allowed her to escape.

"So you saw where they were keeping you."

"One more safe house bites the dust." She grimaced. "Of course, they were long gone by the time I made it to an American checkpoint and could tell them who I was and what I knew."

He reached for her hand, twining his fingers with hers. She let him, grateful for the warmth of his touch. She saw in his dark eyes that he'd guessed what had happened next.

"I was a liability to the CIA at that point," she said aloud. "Since they couldn't trust that I hadn't given up secrets, they reassigned anyone whose cover identity I could have compromised. They changed the location of checkpoints. Alexander Quinn was removed from the Kaziristan station."

"They burned you."

"Not quite as dramatic as people might think, but yeah. I was officially persona non grata at the agency." She looked down at her short, slightly misshapen fingernails and almost laughed. They seemed the perfect metaphor for her life—cut off, tamped down and nowhere near what it used to be.

"Did they give you your new identity?"

She nodded. "They did what they could for me." She touched her cheek, where the exposed nub of her broken tooth had started to ache a little. "I guess I should have expected they'd do something like put a tracker chip in my tooth. They'd want to be sure I wasn't getting into any trouble."

"We sure know how to pick employers, huh?" He flashed a rueful smile.

She found herself smiling in response, even though a moment earlier, her thoughts had been bleak. "Guess we do."

"I should have had Eric look at your tooth while he was here." Rick made a sympathetic face. "Does it hurt?"

"Just a little. I've hurt worse."

His brow furrowed. "Why don't you go back to bed and try to get some rest?"

She sat up straighter, lifting her chin. "I'm fine. I slept all the way here, and I got some sleep last night—"

"On a hard cave floor. And you slept about an hour in the car. Rest." He stood, tugging her hand to pull her to her feet. "At least until dinnertime."

She let him lead her back to the bed, and even allowed him to tuck her in without a peep. But as he started to leave the room, she cleared her voice and called his name.

He turned to look back at her. "Yeah?"

"I can't stay here." The words came out soft and fragile, so she cleared her throat and continued in a stronger voice. "I shouldn't have gone with you back in Thurlow Gap. I put you in danger, and now your family is in danger."

"It won't be the first time," he answered quietly. He turned and walked out of the room.

She leaned back against the pillows, her head starting to ache again. She closed her eyes, not so much to try to sleep as to shut out the homey comfort of Isabel Cooper's guest room.

Rick might think he and his family were prepared for what was coming their way, but Amanda knew better.

Whether her pursuers were rogue MacLear agents, as evidence would suggest—or al Adar sleeper agents who'd somehow slipped into the country undetected—they'd almost certainly followed the satellite signal from the receiver in her porcelain crown. Which meant they weren't working alone.

Someone in the CIA was working with them.

WHEN RICK WALKED OUT the front door, Isabel was sitting at the top of her front porch steps, a glass of iced tea beside her and her slim, jeans-clad legs tucked up nearly to her chest so her feet could rest on the second step down. She picked up the glass and made room for Rick to join her.

He sat beside her, his bones creaking a little. "Thanks for doing this."

"You know a Cooper never turns down a person in need," she answered, a wry tone to her voice.

His little sister had grown a bit cynical over the years. Having their mother walk out of her life when she was still in elementary school hadn't been an auspicious start. But working nearly seven years with the FBI tracking down domestic terrorists and losing her partner, Ben Scanlon, in a bomb blast about five months ago? Rick suspected most of his sister's bleak worldview came as a result of that event.

She hadn't had the heart to stick with the bureau after Scanlon's death. Jesse had convinced her to come home and take her place in the security agency he was building, just as he had with Rick. All of his brothers and sisters were working with Jesse now—Izzy had been the final holdout.

"She wants to leave. Thinks she's putting us in too much danger by sticking around."

Isabel nudged his shoulder with hers. Fortunately, it was the one without the bullet wound. "Is she?"

"Probably," he conceded. He told his sister about the GPS

transmitter in Amanda's crown. "She said a CIA dentist repaired the tooth."

"So you think the CIA sent a black-ops unit to hunt her down?" Isabel sounded skeptical.

"I have no doubt they were tracking her. She and the CIA didn't really part as friends."

"Why not?"

"It's not like the FBI where you can just turn in your notice and go. The CIA is different. You know that." He didn't add what Amanda had told him about her captivity. That was her story to tell.

"Some folks at the FBI weren't all that happy to get my resignation," she murmured regretfully. "I left some investigations in the lurch."

"Are you sure you made the right decision?" His sister didn't seem any happier working for Jesse than she had been working for the bureau.

He knew she was still grieving her partner's death. But had she made things worse by leaving the FBI?

"Rick, you look so tired. Maybe you should go home and get a little rest yourself."

He looked over his shoulder toward the house. His head told him she was right. He hadn't had much sleep since the night before last, and he'd also suffered an injury and a stressful twenty-four hours. He could use a nice big meal and a long night's sleep.

But he didn't like the idea of being very far from Amanda. Not until they knew a lot more about what was going on.

"Okay, how about this?" Isabel said with a grin. "I'll pack a bag and go live at your place for a few days, and you stay here with your ex-girlfriend. Just don't do anything in my house that would make me want to hurl."

He reached over and mussed her hair, making her squawk.

"Brat." As she finger-combed her dark hair, he added, "Are you sure you want to do that?"

"Sure—it'll give me a chance to go through your stuff and learn all your secrets." She shot him a grin that reminded him of what a sneaky little smart aleck she'd been when they were younger. No wonder she'd joined the FBI.

"Okay. I'll take you up on that. You go pack and I'll do the same." He pushed off the steps, grimacing as his injured arm protested.

Before heading back to his house, he stopped at the office to see if Jesse was around. His eldest brother was in his office, going through the day's case reports.

He looked up as Rick entered, his brows lifting slightly at the bedraggled sight of him. "I was wondering if you were going to stop by to tell me what's going on." He waved toward the chair in front of his desk.

Rick sat and looked warily at his brother. "I figured Wade would've caught you up."

"He did, to a degree."

"But you want your pound of flesh?" Rick snapped. He immediately regretted it, but there was no taking it back.

"I'm not trying to bust your chops here. I need to know if there's anything I can do to help." Jesse's expression darkened. "It sounds like your friend has a price on her head, and that could put this company, not to mention our family, in danger."

"You think I don't know that?"

Jesse's lips pressed to a tight line. "Then act like it."

Rick took a deep breath. He didn't know why five minutes with his older brother turned him into an adolescent idiot. "You're right. I'm sorry."

Jesse's expression softened. "How's your arm?"

"Hurts like hell, but I'll live."

"So, is Amanda Caldwell her real name?"

Rick shook his head.

"Do you know what it is?"

"Yeah, but I can't tell you."

"Okay." Jesse reached across the desk and pushed a folded newspaper toward Rick. "This afternoon's paper. Page six."

Rick flipped the paper open and scanned the sixth page. His eyebrow notched upward. "Barton Reid's trial has been postponed?"

"The case seems to be falling apart. Luke and Abby are a little on edge about it."

Rick couldn't blame them. His cousin Luke had just gotten out from under an ongoing death threat from a South American drug lord who'd been hounding him for years. Now he had to contend with the case against Barton Reid going south, which might put him and his wife back in the crosshairs again. Reid had been behind terrorizing Abby to learn what evidence her late husband had found to incriminate Reid.

If he was in the mood for revenge, Abby and Luke were pretty tempting targets.

"I guess the family's rallying the wagons around Gossamer Ridge?" Rick asked aloud.

"That's what Alicia says. Speaking of her—did she catch you when you came in?"

"I didn't see her." Rick's cousin-in-law Alicia had started working for Cooper Security about a month after she married his cousin Gabe. She was a brilliant little dynamo whose PhD in criminal psychology looked very good on the Cooper Security list of credentials. She also happened to be an insightful, natural investigator. They were lucky she'd decided to join the company.

"Well, she'll be looking for you," Jesse told him.

"What does she want?"

"She didn't tell me—just said to let you know she wanted

to see you." Jesse's eyes narrowed. "How much sleep have you had in the last day?"

"A few hours."

"How many of those hours were on the floor of that cave Wade told me about?

"A few," he answered with a wry smile.

"Go home. Get some sleep. We can regroup tomorrow."

Home, Rick thought as he walked back through the bullpen-style communal office where rows of desks, some occupied, some empty, filled the open area. He supposed he and his brothers and sisters all thought of Chickasaw County as home, no matter how far they'd roamed over the years. After all, here they were, all six of them, back in Chickasaw County, all living within a few miles of the sprawling two-story farmhouse where they'd grown up, where their father, now retired, still lived.

But at the moment, the only place that called to him, on a gut-deep level, was his sister Isabel's house.

Because Amanda was there.

He'd thought, as time and distance built between him and those few stolen weeks of fire and feeling, he was over what he'd felt for her.

But clearly, he wasn't.

Maybe it wasn't lovc. Maybe it never had been. But it was more than he'd ever felt for another woman. More than he'd felt, period, for a long while now.

Now he just had to decide what he was going to do about it.

AMANDA HAD COME TO THINK of her captor as an incubus, so thoroughly and horribly had he haunted her dreams for the past three years. In real life, he had seemed far less intimidating, at least on sight. Physically, he was only average in size—tall, perhaps, for a Kaziri, but no more than five foot ten in height, trim and fit but not particularly muscular. He would have been considered pleasant-featured in almost any culture, with handsome brown eyes, high cheekbones and a mobile, laughing mouth. His hair was dark but not black, shot through with russet, especially when the light slanting through the single window in the interrogation room hit it.

His cohort called him Raa Baber—The Tiger.

But in her dreams, as in life, he lacked the noble beauty of the big, sleek cat. The man she knew as The Tiger was hard. Suffocating. Cruel.

She forced herself awake, before the games began. She sat up in the soft bed and threw off the blankets, feeling trapped. Only when she'd scrambled over to the window and let the afternoon light bathe her in reflected warmth did the pounding, rapid-fire cadence of her pulse recede into something approaching normal.

The house was quiet around her, only the faint hum of electricity and her own rapid respirations breaking the silence. She willed herself to relax, to let go of her past for just a few minutes. She was clean—finally—and on the mend. The broth and toast Rick had given her earlier had managed to stay down with no ill effects. And she was, for the moment, safe.

Or so she thought.

Until she heard the front door open.

She supposed most people would assume that Isabel or Rick had returned. It was a logical assumption—the house belonged to Isabel, and Rick had the most interest in where she was and what she was doing.

But Amanda had learned long ago to assume nothing.

She looked around the room for her duffel bag, finding it tucked inside the guest room's small closet. As the sound of footsteps sounded quietly outside her door, she pulled the first spare weapon she could find from within the bag's interior—her SIG Sauer P238. She checked the clip to make sure it was loaded and swung the weapon toward the door as footsteps stopped just outside.

The doorknob rattled. She steadied her weapon.

The door swung open and the intruder took one step inside. It was a woman in her late twenties, with wavy black hair and coffee-black eyes that widened as she spotted the gun in Amanda's hand.

The woman released a soft profanity and lifted her hands, dropping her purse to the floor. "I come in peace," she said quickly. "I'm Alicia Cooper. Rick's cousin Gabe is my husband." She had an accent from somewhere on the West Coast—Oregon, maybe, or northern California.

Amanda didn't drop the weapon. "What do you want?"

"Your help," Alicia answered.

Chapter Nine

Amanda heard more footsteps moving in the house, behind Alicia. The other woman didn't seem to notice, her focus centered on the snub, square nose of the SIG.

"My help?" Amanda asked, wondering if the second person approaching was friend or foe.

"I understand you were attacked yesterday morning by a man who once worked with MacLear."

Amanda's eyes narrowed. How did she know this? "Do you have any ID?"

The footsteps stopped just outside the bedroom door. Once again, the other woman seemed oblivious. "You want to see my driver's license? Really?" There was a surprising hint of delight in her voice. "You still think I'm a threat?"

Amanda shook her head. "You're about as threatening as a three-week-old kitten."

"Don't depend on that. I hear she's dangerous with a baseball bat." Rick's voice preceded him into the bedroom. He arched one eyebrow at the gun still leveled in Amanda's grip. "Put it down. She's one of the good guys."

Amanda slowly lowered the SIG. "She didn't knock."

"I didn't want to wake you if you were asleep," Alicia protested. "Isabel lent me her key. Just thought I'd peek in to see if you were awake."

Her hands shaking a little, Amanda set the SIG on the

bedside table and turned back to look at them, pushing her hair away from her perspiration-damp face. "I'm Amanda."

"Like I said, I'm Alicia Cooper." Alicia flashed her a smile. "How're you feeling?"

"Better," she admitted. She sank onto the end of the bed and gestured toward a nearby chair. "Sit down. Tell me how you want me to help you."

Alicia pulled up the chair and sat in front of her, folding her hands on her lap. She was dressed in a trim-fitting brown trouser suit with a turquoise sweater beneath the jacket. On the outside, she looked calm and composed, yet she seemed to vibrate visibly with pent-up energy. "I understand one of the people who shot at you yesterday was a former MacLear agent."

Amanda glanced at Rick, wondering how much he'd told his family about her background. He met her gaze without flinching, so she guessed he hadn't spilled anything he'd know she wanted to stay a secret.

"Rick's the one who recognized him. I only knew a few MacLear agents, and Rick's the only one I knew well."

"I think it's likely the men who chased you through the forest outside Chattanooga were also MacLear agents."

Rick, who had been hanging back near the doorway, moved forward at Alicia's words, looking at her with interest. He sat next to Amanda on the bed. "Has something happened to make you believe that?"

Alicia nodded. "J.D. put out some calls to old Navy buddies who'd served with Jackson Melville, to see if anyone connected to MacLear had approached them recently about working any new assignments."

"J.D.'s one of my cousins," Rick explained to Amanda. She was beginning to wonder how many Coopers there were.

"A few of them seemed to be evasive in their answers,"

Alicia continued, "while a couple of others were happy to tell him they'd turned down offers of freelance security work because of the taint of any connection to MacLear or Melville."

"Melville can't be involved—he's under indictment," Rick pointed out.

"So is Barton Reid," Alicia countered. "Though that's looking pretty shaky at the moment."

"Nobody reputable is likely to work for Melville or any MacLear upper-level officer again," Rick said firmly.

"Nobody *reputable,*" Amanda agreed quietly. When they both looked at her, she added, "That's the problem, isn't it? MacLear's seedy underbelly has come back out to play."

"Someone has sent them after you," Alicia said with a nod. "It can't be a coincidence that Barton Reid was working at the embassy in Kaziristan while you and Rick were there."

"How do you know so much about Barton Reid?" Amanda asked.

"Jesse hired her specifically to profile Reid," Rick answered for Alicia. "We want to help strengthen the case against him if we can."

"Who's paying Jesse?" Amanda asked.

"Actually, I am," Alicia said with a sheepish grin. "Sort of. I invested in Cooper Security, so when I decided to look into Reid, Jesse was good enough to let me use the company's resources to do it." Her smile widened, this time with pleasure. "He also made me an offer I couldn't refuse—he gave me a job."

"Alicia has a PhD in criminal psychology—"

"And I live here in Chickasaw County," she added. "My husband is a fishing guide on Gossamer Lake. I didn't want him to have to leave his family and the job he loves behind, and I wasn't really looking forward to an hour or more commute to Birmingham, so when Jesse said Cooper Security could use a profiler…" She stopped herself, apparently realizing she was rattling on. Her grin turned sheepish again. "Anyway, I wanted to help Luke and Abby out. They're family. So I'm doing anything I can to get them out from under this constant threat."

Amanda couldn't hold back a slight smile. She might talk a mile a minute, but Alicia Cooper seemed like a decent person with the guts and determination needed to make good things happen for the people around her. Amanda hadn't known too many people like that—they were rare in her world.

"Nailing Barton Reid to the wall will definitely help Luke and Abby," Rick said firmly. "You know I'll help you any way I can, Ali, but the MacLear Special Services Unit was serious about secrecy, especially when it comes to keeping the legitimate end of the company in the dark. I probably know less than you do about what they were up to at this point."

"You may know more than you think," Alicia said. "At the very least, you're familiar with how MacLear worked from the inside out. If we're right about what's going on, some of the SSU agents who escaped detection or managed to slip under the radar have banded together to start their own mercenary force. Guns for hire, with no scruples about who hires them or why."

"And we have to stop them," Rick said, his voice quiet but fierce with determination.

Amanda felt distanced from their conversation. Nothing they were discussing should have had anything to do with her. Not anymore. She'd gotten out, kept her head down, her eyes forward and her mind firmly shut to everything that smacked of her former life.

And yet, here you are, a little voice in her head reminded her. *Recovering from a gunshot wound and running for your life.*

"I'm not sure why rogue SSU agents would be gunning for me," she said aloud.

"Well, the tracker in your tooth suggests a few things—"

Alicia's brow furrowed. "Tracker?"

Rick told her about the tracker they'd found in Amanda's crowned tooth. "The only person who could have implanted the tracker is the person who made the crown, and that was a CIA dentist. So the decision to track her almost certainly came from the CIA."

Alicia winced. "You pulled out your own tooth?"

"I extracted the crown," Amanda corrected. "It didn't really hurt."

"But still!" Alicia grimaced. "All right, you're right about one thing—I can't see how anyone but the CIA could have implanted the tracker. And it really does sound as if the people who were chasing you through Tennessee knew exactly where you were at any given time."

"We never saw their faces," Rick pointed out. "We're assuming they were mercenaries like Delman Riggs—"

"Who?" Alicia asked.

Rick told her about the man Amanda had shot. "He used to be with MacLear—one of the guys the government had tried to indict but ultimately lacked evidence against." He looked at Amanda. "There were several people like that—SSU agents who claimed they were duped and the prosecution couldn't come up with enough evidence for the grand jury to indict."

"But like you said, no decent security firm is going to touch them now," Alicia added. "The taint of MacLear and the allegations against them make them too risky to consider."

"I was lucky I had my brother to fall back on for a job,"

Rick murmured, his voice taut, "and I wasn't ever involved in the shady side of the company."

Amanda saw a flicker of doubt in his eyes, as if he wasn't quite sure he was telling the truth. She tucked that information away for later and addressed the question she'd been wrestling with all day. "I thought the tracker meant the CIA had to be involved. But I don't think the men chasing me were CIA. What went on out there in the woods when they were chasing me was more paramilitary maneuvers than spy craft."

"The CIA has paramilitary units," Alicia pointed out.

"True, but the CIA isn't going to deploy a whole unit of operatives to go after one person who isn't bothering anyone."

"Who would?" Rick asked.

Both Amanda and Alicia turned their gazes to him. "Send a whole unit after me, you mean?" Amanda asked.

He nodded. "You're living under the radar in some tiny mountain town in Tennessee, bothering nobody, like you said. What would compel anyone to send assassins after you? The CIA gave you your identity—have you changed it since then?"

"No."

"Have you moved?"

"No." Amanda's heart sank a little. "Maybe I should have."

"Maybe," Rick conceded. "But the point is—if the CIA wanted you, couldn't they come get you anytime they liked?"

"Maybe Delman Riggs was working for the CIA," Alicia suggested. "It's not like they're always scrupulous about the backgrounds of their hires."

"Still goes back to the same question—why the stealth? The CIA could easily have sent someone you knew well to catch you off guard. Kill you before you could defend yourself."

"And why did Quinn get involved in this?" Amanda asked aloud.

Alicia's brow furrowed. "Who's Quinn?"

Amanda slanted a look at Rick. "Someone we both know."

Alicia's expression cleared. "And on a need-to-know basis, someone I *don't* need to know?"

Rick nodded. "Sorry."

"Should I go?" Alicia asked.

"No, stay," Amanda said, surprising herself. "You said you're a criminal profiler, right?"

"Well, not officially—I mean, there's not really a degree in that—"

"But that's what you do, more or less."

Alicia nodded. "Yeah. That's what I do."

"If you were given my case—multiple attempts on my life—where would you start investigating?"

Alicia thought for a second. "First, I'd find out what you'd been doing most recently. Has your schedule changed at all in the last few weeks?"

"I took some new freelance jobs, but nothing any different from what I've been doing for the last three years."

"Met anyone new?"

"No. I'm not exactly a social butterfly, and Thurlow Gap is a very small place."

As Alicia asked her a series of questions, most of which she quickly answered in the negative, Amanda found her patience wearing thin. Her headache was coming back with a vengeance, and despite Alicia's smart and reasonable questions, she didn't seem to have any better grip on why someone would want her dead, after all this time, than she'd had when she'd first heard Rick give her the assassination code word Alexander Quinn had drummed into her head the day she set foot in Kaziristan.

Thinking of Quinn reminded her of the question she'd asked Rick earlier. Why had Quinn thrown Rick back into her life? What did the old master manipulator know and why was he playing games instead of giving her an overt warning?

"I think the CIA has to be involved somehow." She interrupted Alicia's next question before she got more than a single word out.

"Because of the tracker?" Rick asked.

Amanda glanced at Alicia. "And because of who sent you to my house in the first place."

"Quinn?" Alicia asked.

Amanda and Rick both looked at her. She held up her hands. "Sorry. Need to know. Got it."

"I don't have the highest opinion of the CIA," Rick admitted, "but I don't see them going after you that way."

"What if it wasn't an official thing?" Alicia interjected. "What I mean is, nobody thinks the State Department condoned the things we believe Barton Reid has done, right? Could someone in the CIA be running his own operation, using the rogue MacLear SSU agents?"

Amanda locked gazes with Rick, trying to gauge his reaction. Of course, it was possible there was a corrupt officer running his own game. The CIA was essentially a group of people who kept secrets for a living. Hid their identities, worked in the shadows, told lies as easily as they breathed.

"It's possible," Rick said aloud, echoing her thoughts. "Probable, even."

Alicia nodded. "So the question we should be asking now is, why? They let you leave the agency almost three years ago without kicking up any kind of fight, right?"

"More like the other way around," Amanda murmured,

bitterness aching in her throat. “They were pretty clear that I wasn’t welcome at Langley anymore.”

“Okay, then—what was the last thing you were doing before you were let go?”

Amanda smiled. “I can’t tell you that.”

“Would it help if I pointed out that I’m a psychologist and bound by an ethical code that precludes me from revealing anything you tell me in confidence during a session?”

Amanda’s smile widened more. “You’re incorrigible.”

“I’m serious. I’d be bound to keep your secrets from everyone, including my husband. Which he’ll hate, but he’ll deal.” Alicia leaned forward. “I get it if you don’t want to, but you *can* say whatever you want to me without fear that I’ll reveal it to anyone else.”

The urge to share with someone—anyone—a little of what her life had been like for the past three years was a powerful drive. She forced herself to think before speaking.

“I may want to do that,” she said finally. “But I’d like to speak to Rick alone first.”

Alicia nodded. “No problem.” She stood and headed for the door. “Need me to get you anything? Something to drink?”

“No. I think Rick can do anything I need.” Amanda put a tone of finality in her voice.

She could tell by Alicia’s expression that she understood she was being dismissed. “Rick knows how to reach me.” She gave a goodbye nod and left the room.

Amanda waited until she heard the front door open and close before she turned to Rick. “She’s kind of exhausting.”

“She’s very good at her job, though.”

“I think she may be on to something. About the CIA.”

“Because of Quinn?”

“You know him. He has ears everywhere.”

"He didn't have to be so damn cryptic about it," Rick said flatly. "If he knows something, he should just say it."

"Maybe he doesn't have any evidence. Only suspicions." She knew Rick didn't care much for Quinn, but the man had saved her backside more than once over the course of her time in Kaziristan. He'd been the first person from the CIA to reach her after she escaped al Adar. She'd been hanging by a tiny filament of sanity, and if he hadn't taken her in hand and pulled her from the abyss, she didn't know if she'd still be alive today. "There's one thing I know better than I know my own name—Quinn isn't my enemy."

"But I'm not sure he's your friend, either."

She shook her head. "Probably not."

"He knows what happened to you in Kaziristan, doesn't he?"

"Yeah. He was my handler. He knows everything."

Rick's eyes narrowed. "When I arrived at your house yesterday, you were packed and ready to flee. Was that just because of my call?"

She stood and walked to the window, gazing out on the backyard. The sun was starting to dip in the western sky, the tall pines in the yard casting longer shadows across the newly green grass. Spring had arrived without her noticing, she realized, spotting bright yellow daffodil blooms edging the lawn just below the window. "Quinn sent me something by courier. A box."

"What was in it?"

"Fake fingernails. And a matchbox with your number on it."

Rick made a low grumbling noise in his throat. She turned to look at him and saw his eyes blazing with anger. "If he knows something, he should tell you what it is and stop playing his stupid little spy games."

"What about you?"

His brow rose. "Me?"

"What aren't you telling me?"

He stared at her as if he didn't know what she was talking about. But she could also see confirmation of her suspicions lurking in his dark eyes.

"Earlier, when I was telling you about what happened when al Adar kidnapped me, I saw…something in your eyes. You seemed to react to something I said—about the man al Adar was looking for. They tortured me to get me to reveal his location. They thought I would know."

Rick's dark gaze dropped to the floor. "The Doctor," he said softly.

"You know who he was?"

Rick nodded.

"Did you know *where* he was?"

He looked up at her, pain glittering in his gaze. "Yes."

She crossed back to the bed, her knees feeling wobbly. She sat next to Rick and caught his hand in hers. "Where?"

Regret twisted his features. "With me."

Chapter Ten

Joining MacLear had been a whim, at first. A way to seek the sort of adventure his brother Jesse had found by joining the Marine Corps without actually walking in his brother's footsteps. Jesse had been appalled—his opinion of mercs, as he called them, wasn't positive.

But in his work as a MacLear operative, Rick had found the life he'd thought he wanted. Adventure, travel, enough danger to make life exciting and plenty of variety. He'd also come to believe in what he was doing, a job he saw as a vital support system for the increasingly overextended military units tasked with protecting the world from the constant and escalating threat of conflagration.

Learning MacLear was a high-priced facade for dangerous adventurism had been one hell of a blow to his sense of purpose. But it hadn't been the first.

Losing Amahl Dubrov had been the beginning of the end of his association with MacLear.

"I was one of three MacLear agents given the job of protecting a Kaziri doctor," he said aloud from his position near the window, where he'd fled to avoid looking into her pained blue eyes. "They told me his name was Amahl Dubrov. Kaziri mother, Russian father."

"They never told me his name." Her voice was faint and

faraway. Was she reliving that time in captivity? Were his words dragging her back through her memories of captivity?

"I had the night shift. It should have been the easier shift—Dubrov usually slept like a baby, and the guard duty took place during the middle of summer, so nighttime was about the only bearable time of day."

"Why were you guarding him?"

He slanted a quick look her way. She sat on the edge of the bed, looking not at him but at some invisible point on the far wall. He suspected she was back in Kaziristan in her mind, seeing and smelling and hearing all the things she'd probably spent the past three years running from.

"They never told me. Just said he was valuable to both the good guys and the bad guys, and it was our job to make sure the bad guys didn't get him."

"Did you speak to him?"

"Of course. But we were told not to ask questions, and he didn't seem particularly eager to make friends."

"What did he look like?"

Rick closed his eyes, trying to conjure the distant memory. "He was medium height—five-seven or -eight? Black, wavy hair. He wore it short, but you could tell that if it grew out, it would be wavy. Maybe even curly."

"What color eyes?"

"Mismatched," he remembered with a start, surprised he'd forgotten about that small fact until now. "One brown eye, one hazel-green eye. Very striking."

He heard a soft puff of air escape her throat. Turning, he found her looking at him.

"Did he have a scar over his left eyebrow?"

"Yes." He narrowed his eyes. "You know who he was."

She nodded. "I'm almost certain the man you knew as The Doctor was Abbadi Kurash. Dubiq Kurash's oldest son."

Rick considered her theory. Except for the mismatched

eyes, the man he knew as Amahl hadn't looked much like old Dubiq Kurash, the flamboyant and charismatic democratic reformer who had led the Kaziri Democratic Union's opposition to the corrupt Barvani regime. But as the disparate pieces of the puzzle began to click into place, he realized that Amanda could be right about Amahl Dubrov's real identity.

At the time of the embassy siege that had set off the country's democratic uprising, the Kaziri Democratic Union had been al Adar's primary rival in filling the vacuum left by Barvani's fall. But Dubiq had died of a stroke just a couple of months before Rick had been tasked with guarding the mysterious Dr. Dubrov. Had both the Kaziri Democratic Union and al Adar seen Abbadi Kurash as his father's political heir?

"Maybe the KDU hired MacLear to protect Kurash Junior while the uprising was in full swing," he said aloud.

"That might explain why al Adar was willing to torture me to find out where he was." Amanda nibbled her lower lip, her expression thoughtful. "But why me? I wasn't connected to the section at the CIA that was handling the KDU."

A horrible thought flickered through Rick's mind. "What if it was because of me?"

"You think they knew you were guarding Dubrov?"

"I had started guarding him less than a week before we ended things between us." The new assignment was part of the reason he didn't fight hard to convince her not to walk away. He knew his evenings would be occupied and there would be no time to be with her.

He'd assumed he'd have a second chance with her, once the assignment was over. He could track her down and convince her to forget about the rules. But by the time things with Dubrov went wrong, she had disappeared. He'd thought she'd asked for reassignment.

He'd been wrong.

"And if they'd found out the two of us were involved—" She broke off, her lips flattening to a thin line.

"They might have thought you knew more about my job than you did." He leaned toward her, putting his hand over hers where they lay clasped tightly in her lap. "I'm so sorry. If they went after you because of me—"

Her gaze lifted to meet his. "Maybe we're wrong. If they knew we were seeing each other, then clearly they were able to keep tabs on one or both of us. Which means they could have followed you at any time to wherever you were keeping Dubrov."

He shook his head. "I never really tried to evade detection when I was meeting you. I didn't care who knew. That was always more important to you than to me." He shot her a wry smile. "But we had several layers of precautions in dealing with Dubrov. For one thing, we moved him constantly, sometimes as many as two or three times a night if the pressure was on. We had to pass through three or four MacLear perimeter checkpoints to reach him—and if anyone had followed us, those perimeter guards would have spotted them."

"What happened to Abbadi Kurash?" she asked suddenly. "I don't keep up with much news out of Kaziristan, but I do know he never ran for office or did anything with the KDU movement."

Rick's gut twisted. "Four weeks into our assignment, our perimeter was breached. Massive security failure. When the guards missed a check-in, we thought something had gone wrong. We radioed our unit leader, who told us to stay put."

"Stay put? In a situation like that?" Amanda looked incredulous. "That's all sorts of wrong."

"I knew that at the time, but I'd been given my orders." The roiling sensation in his midsection grew stronger at the memory. "I should have listened to my own instincts."

"Who gave the order?"

"A guy named Salvatore Beckett." He wondered if she'd recognize the name.

Apparently not. "Didn't you raise the question of his reckless order to stay put?" she asked, sounding indignant.

"Of course I did. I was told Beckett was sacked. But he actually was reassigned to the Special Services Unit."

Amanda sighed. "Them again."

"I think the Dubrov ambush may have been his audition," Rick admitted, voicing the growing conviction that had nagged him ever since he'd learned, along with the rest of the world, that MacLear had built a unit that was nothing more than guns for hire to the highest bidder, ideology be damned.

"How do you know he was in the SSU?"

"Remember what the SSU did to my cousin and his wife?"

She nodded.

"Salvatore Beckett was one of the MacLear agents my cousins captured a year and a half ago. Barton Reid sent them to hunt down Luke's son, Stevie, to use him to blackmail Luke and Abby into giving them the evidence Abby's first husband had gathered against them." Only the grit and determination of his cousins had stopped the unit from achieving its goal.

"You think MacLear set up the ambush in some way?"

"Probably took money to let it happen."

"What happened to Kurash?"

"We were surrounded. They came in guns blazing. The other agent working with me was killed. I was hit in the back of the head by a bullet, but it hit at a strange angle and glanced off the bone without penetrating. Knocked me out, and I guess they figured me for dead. When I came to, The Doctor was gone."

Amanda pressed her fingertips to her forehead, as if she was in pain. He scooted his chair closer, touching her knee. She looked up at his touch, her eyes wide and dark. "Too close," she said softly, one hand dropping away from her head to touch his face.

Her fingers were cold, but somehow they left a trail of fire as they brushed across the curve of his jaw. He felt his whole body quicken, as if he hadn't felt so exhausted just seconds earlier that he thought he might sleep a week.

Her other hand joined the first, cradling his face between her palms. "What day was it that you woke to find Kurash gone?"

"March eighteenth." Almost three years ago, he realized. In some ways, it seemed a lifetime ago. And sometimes, it felt as if it had happened only yesterday.

"March eighteenth," she repeated, her lips curving in a faint smile.

"Does that mean something?"

"That's the day I escaped al Adar." She pressed her forehead to his. "Most of the men disappeared that day, leaving me alone with only a single guard. The perfect guard for my purposes," she added. "Malid wasn't hard to outwit, and he was too slow and lumbering to catch me when I got free."

She'd told him this story before, but he felt the same fresh flood of relief, as if he'd just heard the news of her escape for the first time. Blindly, he reached for her, pulling her into his arms.

She wrapped her arms around him, sliding into his lap. Her lips brushed the side of his jaw, setting off brushfires along his nerve endings.

"I'm sorry for what happened to Abbadi Kurash," she whispered, "but I'm not sorry I'm still alive." There was a strange fervor in her voice, an intensity that made him draw back from her so he could see her face.

Her face glowed with life, her eyes blazing with internal fire, and his breath caught in his chest.

This was the woman he'd known in Kaziristan. Full of strength and passion.

He cradled her face between his hands. "There you are," he murmured.

She didn't ask what he meant. He supposed she knew even better than he did how different she'd become.

He bent his head to kiss her, but she pulled back from him, just far enough to speak. "I've been thinking about something Alicia said."

He sighed, drawing back to look at her. "What's that?"

"That I could trust her to keep my secrets. Is that true?"

Rick thought about it for a moment, not wanting to jump into anything that might put her life in greater danger. He'd been working with Alicia for a few months now, and she was conscientious and honorable. If she promised to keep a secret, he believed she would.

"Yes. It is," he said finally. "And you know who else you can trust? My family. There's not a single one of them who'd ever do anything to put your life in danger."

She smiled again. "I don't remember you having such warm feelings about your brother Jesse a few years ago."

He grimaced. "Jesse and I didn't see eye to eye about my working for MacLear. He thought I should have joined the Marine Corps like he did. Like my brother Wade did later."

"And now he owns a private security company like MacLear," she said with a wry smile.

He shook his head. "Not like MacLear. Jesse is nothing like Jackson Melville. My brother and I don't agree on everything, even now. But I would trust him with any of my deepest secrets." He met her gaze with conviction. "I'd trust him with any of yours."

She cupped his jaw with her palm. “You’re lucky to have family like that.”

She’d never told him anything about her own family situation, of course. Knowing she was a CIA operative, he’d never expected her to. He wasn’t sure he could expect her to tell him anything now, either. But he couldn’t help wondering why she seemed so utterly alone in the world.

What kind of background must she have had to cut herself off so willingly and completely from her family?

“Let’s do it,” she said.

He leaned toward her, his voice a low growl. “Do it?”

She smiled, pressing her fingertips against his mouth. “Slow down, big boy. I meant, let’s talk to your family.”

He drew back again, studying her face. “Are you sure?”

“Are you?”

He nodded. “You can trust them all.”

JESSE COOPER LEANED BACK in his desk chair, his gaze directed toward the panoramic scene outside the wide plate-glass window of his second-floor office. Waning sunlight cast deepening shadows across the gently sloping landscape leading down to Gossamer Creek. If he followed the meandering waterway to the south, he could reach Gossamer Lake within ten miles. Beyond the creek, there was a steep drop-off, giving him an unimpeded view of Chickasaw Valley. The breathtaking panorama of rolling farmland and wooded wilderness made his office the envy of everyone who worked at Cooper Security.

None of his family had seemed to worry much about how he’d been able to afford the large, modern office space so soon after deciding to open Cooper Security. He supposed his reputation within the family for being the straight shooter had been enough to forestall any questions that might have occurred to them.

He wasn't thrilled with keeping things from them, in truth, but when he'd taken on this job, he'd agreed to certain terms.

Absolute discretion was one of the biggest.

The phone on his desk rang, the call coming in directly to his phone, bypassing the switchboard. He never worried about the phone ringing while he was away—Heller never called on the landline unless Jesse called first. And Jesse never called unless it was an emergency.

He wondered if Maddox Heller would consider Amanda Caldwell's arrival an emergency.

He answered on the third ring. "Cooper."

"Which one?" asked the low Georgia drawl on the other end of the line.

"The sane one," Jesse answered with a grin.

"I didn't know there were any," Maddox Heller zinged him.

"Funny."

"What you got?"

Jesse told his old friend about Amanda Caldwell's arrival and what Rick had told him of their ordeal in Tennessee. "Looks like MacLear's SSU has reconstituted itself on the down low."

"Damn," Heller murmured. "I really thought we were shed of those cockroaches."

"Guess we'll have to get back to stomping on them one at a time," Jesse replied. "But the more pressing question is, what do they want from this woman?"

"What do you know about her?"

"She's someone my brother knew when he was working for MacLear in Kaziristan. Nobody's said so, but I get the feeling she might have been CIA. I don't have any contacts with the company, but I figured you might."

"One or two," Heller admitted. "Let me do some asking around."

"Thanks." Jesse heard the sound of a child's voice over the line. "Is that your kid?"

"Yeah, Iris is working at the greenhouse today, so I'm watching Daisy. I swear, that baby's grown an inch since she got out of bed this morning."

Jesse felt a twinge of envy. He'd had a chance, once, to be a husband and father. He'd chosen the Marine Corps instead. For the most part, he didn't regret the choice. But once in a while, something like the sound of Maddox Heller's daughter laughing on the other end of the line brought home the things he'd given up for his service to his country.

"Give me a day. Then call me and I'll check back in with what I've learned," Heller said.

"Thanks. I owe you one."

"Cooper, what you're doin' for me outweighs anything I can do for you. I know what it cost you when I asked you to do it. I'm not likely to forget that anytime soon."

"It's not the big sacrifice I thought it would be," Jesse admitted, turning away from the window. He was finding his work at Cooper Security more satisfying than he'd imagined he could. It was still service, after all.

Without the government middleman.

AMANDA HAD STIPULATED only a couple of ground rules. First, she would talk only to Coopers. None of the other agents at Cooper Security were invited to the powwow. And second, she wanted to have the meeting at Isabel's house. For whatever reason, she'd begun to think of the rambling old farmhouse as a sanctuary, the first place she'd felt safe in a long time.

How much of that sense of security was a result of having Rick constantly by her side, she didn't want to contemplate.

She was relieved that the Cooper siblings began arriving before her jittery hormones could escalate the sexual tension between her and Rick.

She'd like to think she was wise enough to keep her wits about her, especially in the middle of a dangerous situation still developing. But now, as during the time they'd spent together in Kaziristan, she found herself in grave danger of losing control when Rick was around. She'd taken far too many chances when they were sneaking around Tablis in search of places to be alone and give in to their mutual passion.

She had to be smarter now than she had been then.

Isabel had arrived first, with food, the unmistakable aroma of smoked pork wafting all the way to the bedroom, drawing Amanda to the kitchen. She found Isabel at the counter, pulling takeout boxes out of a huge bag emblazoned with a bright red logo that read Billy's Pit Stop.

"Hope you're not a vegetarian," Isabel said with a grin.

"If I were, the smell coming out of those boxes would convert me," Amanda replied with an answering smile. "What can I do to help?"

"Sit down and keep me company. You need to be resting."

"Please, don't mommy me," Amanda growled in frustration. "I'm feeling so much better, and I'm ready to pitch in and do my part." She leveled her gaze with Isabel. "Of everything."

Isabel nodded slowly, her smile fading. "I know how frustrating it can be when you're sidelined."

Amanda caught a glimpse of the sadness she'd seen in Isabel's eyes earlier. This time, she couldn't quell her curiosity. "You were sidelined?"

Isabel sighed. "Permanently, I guess. I was put on desk duty at the FBI after my partner was murdered in a bombing a few months ago. I just didn't have the heart to be micromanaged when I wanted to be out looking for his killer." Her lips thinned with irritation. "Insubordination doesn't go over very well in Washington."

"So you didn't quit?"

"Oh, I quit," she said with a nod. "But only because I saw the termination coming." Isabel was saved from any further explanation by the sound of the front door opening. She shot a wry look at Amanda. "Family never knocks."

A slim, wiry-looking woman in her late twenties entered the room, carrying a couple of plastic jugs of tea, one in each hand. She had wavy auburn hair, storm cloud–gray eyes and a spattering of freckles across the bridge of her nose. Despite the different coloring, there was enough resemblance between the newcomer and Isabel for Amanda to assume this was another of Rick's sisters.

"Amanda, this is my sister Megan. Meggie, this is Amanda."

Megan set the jugs of tea on the counter and smiled at Amanda. "Nice to meet you, finally."

Amanda made a mental note to ask Rick just how much he'd told his family about her. "Same here."

"Shannon's on the way," Megan told Isabel, reaching up into the overhead cabinet and bringing down several drinking glasses. "That's our younger sister," she added for Amanda's benefit, flashing a wicked smile. "The baby of the family. Prepare for a display of merciless teasing."

"She's twenty-six, but feel free to treat her like she's still in high school," Isabel said. "We all do."

"I'm feeling lucky to be an only child," Amanda murmured.

"Oh, it's not all unrelenting cruelty," Megan said with a laugh. "Let an outsider mess with any one of us and there's hell to pay from all of us."

"I'm kind of counting on that," Amanda admitted.

"Rick asked Alicia to come, too," Isabel said. "I know she's not strictly part of our family—"

"Cousins-in-law are in the gray zone," Megan agreed.

"—but we all agreed that she can offer something we can't," Isabel finished.

Amanda arched an eyebrow. "Such as?"

"She's a licensed hypnotherapist," Megan answered.

Amanda felt a flutter of alarm. "And that's good because?"

The two sisters exchanged quick looks before Isabel turned to Amanda and spoke in a low, serious tone. "Because we think you should undergo hypnosis."

Chapter Eleven

Rick arrived at Isabel's house just as Alicia was driving up. He joined her on the flagstone walkway, eyeing her with a little curiosity. He hadn't invited her to the family conference, wanting to ease Amanda into the circle of family trust one step at a time.

"Surprised to see me?" she asked.

"Not because I think you shouldn't be here—"

"But you didn't want to overwhelm Amanda?" she guessed accurately. At his nod, she added, "I figured that."

"So who invited you?"

"Megan and Isabel."

"Do I want to know why?" They had reached the front door of the farmhouse. As Alicia started to knock, Rick forestalled her, opening the door without the formality of an invitation. "Family," he said with a wry grin.

"Yeah, still having to get used to you Southern people and your quaint ways," Alicia answered in a low, equally wry tone.

They found Amanda in the kitchen with Isabel and Megan. Tension floated through the air, as tangible as the mouthwatering aroma of barbecue.

"You told her already?" Alicia eyed Rick's two sisters, who looked both guilty and annoyed.

"They did," Amanda answered for them, her eyes flashing cold blue fire.

"Told her what?" Rick moved to Amanda's side.

Isabel's eyebrows lifted slightly at his show of solidarity with the outsider. "That we think she should consider hypnotic regression," she answered, her tone defensive.

"Why would they think I need that?" Amanda turned her baleful gaze on Rick, suspicion shining in her eyes.

"I have no idea." He hadn't mentioned a word to anyone in his family about what Amanda had experienced in Kaziristan, which is the only event she might need help remembering. He looked at his sisters for an explanation.

"It was my suggestion," Megan admitted quietly, drawing Amanda's fiery gaze to her.

"Why?" Amanda demanded. "What do you think I need to remember that I don't already?"

Megan glanced at Rick, then back at Amanda. "A couple of years ago, I was working on a three-state Homeland Security task force, studying the rise in incidents of domestic terrorism. One of the things we were given was a list of potential threats. Citizens who, for one reason or another, might be motivated to act against the federal government in a violent way."

Rick stared at his sister in surprise. "Are you saying—?"

"Amanda was on the list." Megan's gray eyes were gentle as she took a step around the counter toward Amanda. "We weren't told all the details of what happened to you in Kaziristan. Just that something had, and that your loyalties may have been compromised in some way by events there."

Amanda uttered a low profanity and turned away from them.

Rick rounded on his sister. "I asked her to trust us, and you ambush her? Thanks a lot."

"It's not an ambush," Isabel said in a firm, quiet tone.

"Nobody here believes Amanda is a potential terrorist threat."

Amanda whirled around. "Then why hypnosis? You need one last bit of proof that I'm not a terrorist?"

"It's not about proving anything," Alicia interceded. "It's about helping you remember more about what happened to you."

"Why?" Rick asked, sliding his arm around Amanda's trembling shoulders. A surge of fire poured through him as he felt her lean against his side. "Why should she relive that?"

"Because there must be a reason someone's after her now after leaving her alone for three years," Megan answered.

Amanda pulled away from Rick's embrace. Her chin rose, reminding him that for all the trauma she'd gone through in the past three years, she was still the strong, brilliant woman who'd first caught his eye on a street in Tablis.

When she spoke, her voice was steady, her words a statement of fact, not a question. "And the best chance of learning that reason is to find out what really happened to me in Kaziristan."

NOW THAT SHE'D AGREED to the hypnosis, Amanda was surprised to discover her only emotion was relief. As unpleasant as she might find the idea of digging into that part of her past, she couldn't deny the logic that had led Megan to the suggestion. If nothing else, Alexander Quinn's initial cryptic message—the box with the fake fingernails—had suggested a direct Kaziristan connection to the threat coming her way.

She found a certain sense of freedom, too, in being able to release the feelings, fears and memories she'd spent so long holding locked inside her, where they had festered until her soul had become infected with doubt and fear. It would be good to let go of those emotions. Maybe then she could rediscover the woman she had been before.

The woman she wanted to be again.

She could tell Rick didn't share her sense of relief. He paced the floor in front of the chair where she sat, his brow furrowed with worry. "You don't have to do this. My family shouldn't have ganged up on you that way."

She caught his hand as he made another pass in front of her, stilling his movement. "They didn't force me to do this. I need to."

He gazed down at her with eyes as dark as the night that had fallen outside the window. "Hypnosis might make you remember things you don't want to."

He was still afraid there were things she hadn't told him. If she'd had missing pieces of her memory, she might worry the same thing. But she hadn't lost consciousness. She hadn't been incapacitated, despite the torment.

She knew what had—and hadn't—happened to her.

But if hypnosis could help her remember forgotten details about her captors, then there was a chance she'd discover the missing clue that would explain why she'd become someone's target so long after her escape.

"I need to do this," she told him softly.

From the hallway, the sound of voices gave them a little warning that their quiet cocoon was about to be invaded. She let go of Rick's hand and he stepped away, claiming a seat on the ottoman at her feet and pasting on a smile as his brothers and sisters entered. While he and Amanda escaped to the living room after dinner, they'd stayed in the kitchen to wash up.

Considering they'd used paper plates and plastic utensils at dinner, Amanda suspected the other Coopers had stayed in the other room to give Rick and Amanda a moment alone to discuss the coming hypnosis session. It hadn't been necessary for her—she'd made her decision. But maybe Rick had needed the time to regroup, for he seemed less tense now than he had just a few minutes earlier.

His youngest sister, Shannon, ruffled his hair as she passed him to take a seat on the end of the sofa, making Amanda smile. She was a tall, coltish woman in her mid-twenties, with dark hair and bright brown eyes. She resembled her sister Isabel, except for the splash of light freckles across her nose that reminded Amanda of red-haired Megan's Irish complexion.

The room was small, and all the Coopers perching on any available flat surface only made it seem smaller. If Amanda were prone to claustrophobia, she might be climbing the wall, but to her surprise, she found an odd sense of comfort sitting there surrounded by Coopers.

Rick's eldest brother, Jesse, was the last to enter the room. Unlike the others, he chose not to sit, standing instead in front of the group as if he'd called a meeting to order.

He had come as a surprise to Amanda. She supposed his status as the elder brother had made her expect a man who looked bigger than life, but Jesse Cooper turned out to be a whipcord-lean man of average height with a quiet demeanor and watchful eyes the color of dark chocolate.

Rick had asked earlier where their father, Roy, was. He'd looked a little dismayed when Jesse told him that the elder Cooper was on a fishing trip to Texas with their uncle Mike, probably because that left Jesse as the de facto head of the family.

The tension between Jesse and Rick had been immediately obvious in the wary looks exchanged between them, a tension that didn't exist between Rick and his other siblings. Jesse was another secret-keeper, she'd realized right away. A man who had a whole life going on beneath the placid surface of his outer facade.

But were those hidden depths a threat to her? Or an untapped source of help?

She wasn't sure. But she was tired of running, tired of looking for ulterior motives behind every act of kindness. If Jesse Cooper was planning to betray her, then he'd be betraying his family, as well, for the rest of the Coopers seemed open, friendly and eager to help her out.

"Will tomorrow morning around eleven be too soon? For the hypnosis session, I mean." Alicia spoke first, despite Jesse's commanding presence at the front of the room. Amanda felt her nerves jerk at the unexpected sound of her voice.

"Tomorrow at eleven should be fine."

"Are there any particular questions I should ask?" This time, Alicia's question seemed to be directed more toward the other Coopers than toward Amanda.

"I'll brief you first thing in the morning," Jesse said.

Amanda looked up at him. "What do you know about what I went through?"

He turned his cool, dark gaze to her. "What Megan told me about the Homeland Security report."

Amanda wasn't sure he was being completely honest, but she decided to pretend she was. "I can't imagine the CIA spilled all their secrets in a report," she answered with matching calm. She looked at Alicia. "Is there any way for me to direct the session? Will I be aware enough to do that?"

"I pretty much believe all hypnosis is self-hypnosis," Alicia answered with a wry smile. "You're focusing your attention inward. I can make suggestions to help you keep your focus, but if you have something particular in mind that you want to explore, you can certainly do that."

"Good. I think that's how I want to handle it." She looked at Jesse again. "The CIA would never have put the details of what happened to me in a Homeland Security report."

"Do you want to be alone with me, or do you want someone with you?" Alicia asked.

Amanda looked into Rick's worried eyes as she answered Alicia. "Everyone will hear it anyway, right? I mean, you'll be recording the session—"

"That was the plan," Alicia agreed.

"Then I'll be there with her," Rick said in a raspy voice. "If you want me to be," he added in a lower tone to Amanda.

"I do."

He gave a nod, though she could see dread in his eyes.

"Then we're set." Jesse's tone suggested the meeting had come to an end.

As if on cue, all of Rick's siblings started moving, stopping where she sat to say their goodbyes. Only Isabel stuck around—it was her house, after all. She saw the others out, giving Alicia and Rick another minute alone.

"You should go home and get some rest. Tomorrow may be a long day."

He slid the ottoman closer so that he could touch her face. "This is home. Isabel's trading houses with me for a few days."

She arched an eyebrow.

"I don't want to leave you alone."

"Isabel would be here."

He didn't answer, but she could see in his eyes the real reason he didn't want to leave her here with his sister.

"You think I'm going to run the second your back's turned."

"And if I leave you here with Isabel, you're not going to hare off and make me chase after you again?"

She supposed he had reason to doubt her. She'd already run once. And staying here, trusting him and his family, felt like a huge gamble.

She hadn't been a gambler in a long, long time.

"You don't have to worry," she promised. Unless something happened between now and later to make her believe that leaving was safer than staying.

His knowing half smile made her feel uncomfortably certain he'd just read her mind. He bent closer, until his lips brushed against her ear. "If you run, take me with you this time."

A shiver ran down her body, sparking sizzles of awareness along her nerves. His lips brushed her ear again, but this time he said nothing, just pressed a light kiss against the lobe.

His lips traced the tendon down the side of her neck, settling warm and soft against the curve of her collarbone, his tongue brushing the skin over that ridge of bone.

Her sex contracted, making her clutch at his arms just to stay upright. Beneath her fingers, she felt the bulge of the gauze bandage under his sleeve a half second before his breath exploded against her throat in a hiss of pain.

She pulled back. "I'm sorry, I didn't mean—"

He laughed softly, though pain had brought moisture to his eyes. "We're a sad pair with our matching gunshot wounds, aren't we?" He touched the furrow between her eyes. "Maybe we should take it as a sign it's time to hit the sack."

Wrong choice of words, Amanda thought, memories scorching her mind. Seeing his dark eyes dilate until they were as black as ink, she knew the same memories were blazing their way into his mind, as well.

"Separately," he added with a wry smile that didn't manage to drive the feral hunger from his gaze. "If you want."

She wanted to take him into her bed, to open her thighs and take him into her. She wanted to ride the waves of desire until a riptide of pleasure pulled her into its relentless undertow.

She wanted to forget the years that had passed since she last lost herself in his arms.

The sound of Isabel walking down the hallway, her footsteps clicking against the polished hardwood floor, snapped the exquisite cord of tension stretching between them. Rick pulled back, letting cool air fill the heated space between their bodies. His legs seemed to shake as he pushed to his feet to face his sister.

"Rick, I've been thinking about our offer to trade places."

"And you've changed your mind?" He sounded disappointed. Amanda hid a smile.

"Actually," Isabel said, "I'm not sure it's a good idea for either of us to stay there."

Rick turned in the doorway. "Why not?"

"I know they were probably tracking Amanda through the device in her crown." She shot Amanda an apologetic look. "Which reminds me, we need to make sure we fix that crown for you tomorrow. I know it's got to be hurting you."

"Not too bad, but I'll remind you."

"Good. But back to the tracker—if they know who Amanda is, it's possible they know who you are, too."

"And you think they might come looking for me at home?"

"Exactly. You've got your home wired with security, so we can monitor for any intruders. But I don't think it's smart for me to stay there alone."

"I guess I can take the sofa." He looked skeptically at the piece of furniture, which didn't look long enough to be comfortable for Amanda, much less for Rick.

"Nah, you can take my bed," Isabel said quickly. "Tonight, at least. I'm going to Huntsville tonight."

"Huntsville? Why?"

"I'm giving a presentation at a writer's convention in Fort Payne next month—Jesse thinks it would be good PR. I'm meeting the conference chair in Huntsville first thing in the morning to discuss what they want from me, so I'm grabbing a room at a motel there so I won't have to worry about morning traffic. I've already packed a bag, and I need to head out now so I can get there in time to settle in before bedtime." Isabel headed for her bedroom. "I'll try to be back in time for the hypnosis session. For moral support."

Rick's gaze remained locked with Amanda's. She found him hard to read, though she wasn't sure whether it was because he was trying to hide his thoughts from her or because his emotions were in such turmoil that she couldn't see past the chaos.

He started to walk Isabel out when she emerged from her room, but she waved him off. "See you tomorrow around eleven."

The front door closed behind her, the lock engaged with a rasp of metal on metal and Amanda and Rick were alone.

Completely alone.

Amanda's ears rang with the silence left in Isabel's wake. She felt a sudden, jittery urge to fill the silence, though at the moment, she didn't know what to say or do.

Or how to feel.

Leave it to Rick Cooper, with his characteristic blunt honesty, to get right to the heart of things. He turned to her, his eyes blazing. "I want you. You know that, right?"

She nodded, her chest aching. "But it can't happen."

"I tell myself that, too, but I don't believe it."

"Then I believe it for you. All we ever had was sex, Rick. You know it. I know it—"

"That's all we allowed ourselves to have," he said in a voice as rough as sandpaper. "We never tried something different."

"We didn't want anything different." Feelings were messy, and Kaziristan had already been too messy a place, too volatile a situation, to allow their feelings to make things that much harder for them.

Her life was too up in the air even now for her to think about anything but two bodies pressed together in the dark. Considering more—wanting more—was folly.

"I did," he said. "I do."

As she rose to her feet, he closed the distance between them in a couple of steps. But he didn't touch her. She felt the heat of him, as warm and vibrant as a caress, but he kept his hands resolutely by his side.

"You want more, too. I can see it in your eyes."

She lowered her gaze, feeling naked.

"You can tell yourself you just want to use my body to make you forget the rest of the craziness in your life. But it's not true." He finally touched her, a light brush of his fingers against the bare skin of her wrist. His voice dipped to a silky growl. "I think you're ready to stick around and see where things take us—"

"I can't," she whispered, the words burning like bile in her throat. She pulled away from him, her chest tightening as she scurried to the guest bedroom. "I'm sorry."

She escaped into the bedroom and shut the door behind her, acid tears stinging her eyes. Groping her way through the darkened bedroom, she bumped into the mattress with her knees and fell onto the bed, pressing her hot cheeks against the cool sheets.

I can't, she thought, the words blazing a bright, hot path through the darkness behind her eyes. *I can't I can't I can't—*

The constriction in her chest eased, and the frantic chanting in her head finally stilled, but the ache in her soul remained. She rolled onto her back and stared at the ceiling, where moonlight played tag with shadows across the drywall.

She had been ten years old when she'd walked into her mother's bedroom in the middle of the night after a bad dream and realized all those uncles her mother brought home to visit were really just men she had sex with. It hadn't been long after that she'd walked in on that gory scene in the kitchen.

She lost her virginity at sixteen in the back of a football player's car. She lost the last of her romantic illusions the next day when every guy on the team knew what had happened, and her gridiron Romeo let her know in the cruelest terms possible that she was nothing more than a warm, willing body to him.

After that, she'd set her own terms. She had sex when she wanted to, with whom she wanted to, and she walked away whenever she was good and damned ready. What she didn't do was pretend two bodies creating friction in the night had anything to do with love and commitment and forever.

Forever was for other people. She was lucky if she made it through right now.

Only Rick had ever made her believe sex could be something more. And even he had left her when she'd most needed him to look past her bravado and cool logic to see the hunger for forever that burned in her soul like a wildfire.

For almost three years, she'd buried that fire beneath layers of stony determination and constant fear.

And buried was where it would stay.

Chapter Twelve

"How are you feeling? You still okay?" Alicia sounded distant, almost like a voice in the back of her mind. Amanda knew she was supposed to be in a hypnotic state, knew she probably was, but it just felt as if she were very relaxed, as if all the stresses and worries that had haunted her for the past few years had taken a vacation, leaving her clearheaded for the first time in a long time.

They had gotten past her initial abduction, which had turned out to be much less painful in the reliving than she'd thought. They were talking about her primary captor now.

Amanda had told the CIA everything she could remember about The Tiger at the time of her escape, relating her fears about his possible goals. Her handlers had sworn to look into everything she'd told them.

She had no reason to doubt they had, did she? She couldn't imagine Alexander Quinn, for all his secrecy and manipulations, would turn his back on the possibility of a high-value terrorist target who posed a threat to the U.S.

But Quinn hadn't been at that debriefing, she realized. He'd been on an assignment.

"Are you remembering something?" Rick's voice jarred her concentration, making her jump. She clung to the thread of focus, keeping her eye on The Tiger, whose calm brown eyes seemed locked with hers in a deadly stare-off.

Did he remember her as clearly as she now remembered him?

"I can identify The Tiger if I ever see him again," she said aloud, not voicing the sudden flicker of doubt she'd just had about the CIA. "I never could before."

"What about the others?" Rick asked this question again, his voice closer.

Amanda gave up trying to stick with her focus. He was too close. She could feel the heat of his body, smell the masculine essence, unique to him, that had once been as familiar to her as the sound of her own voice. She opened her eyes and found him only a few inches away from where she sat on the sofa, his worried gaze tangling with hers.

"They're not important," she said with conviction, suddenly certain she'd found an important key to unraveling the mystery behind the recent attempts on her life. "The Tiger is. And the sooner I speak to a sketch artist, the better."

"I'll call Cissy," Alicia said, already on the move. "She's home on spring break."

Rick pulled up the ottoman and sat at Amanda's knees, reaching out to curl his hand around hers. "Are you sure?"

"I'm sure," she said. She couldn't describe it, not aloud, but she could still sense The Tiger's gaze, locked with hers in a battle of wills. She'd spent the past three years running from the battle, too weary and injured and raw to arm herself and enter the fray.

But The Tiger had never laid down his arms. She felt it, bone deep. He saw her as a threat, and for some reason, at this point in time, he'd decided to end the battle—end the threat—once and for all.

The ruthless, soulless MacLear rogues who'd tried to kill her might be the blade of the sword, but she was now thoroughly convinced it was The Tiger who was wielding it.

RICK'S YOUNG COUSIN Cissy worked with Amanda for a good half hour, listening carefully to Amanda's directions while she sketched. Finally, Amanda said, "That's him." She turned to Rick, gesturing for him to join them. "Do you recognize him?"

Rick studied the sketch his young cousin had drawn. The man pictured was average-looking. Pleasant, ordinary features. He supposed the fellow pictured would be considered a moderately attractive man. But there was nothing noteworthy about him. Rick could have passed him on the streets of Tablis dozens of times and never really noticed him.

He met Amanda's watchful gaze and shook his head. "I'm sorry. No."

"There's an intensity about his gaze that is impossible to capture unless you've seen it." Amanda smiled at Cissy, who carefully tore the page from her sketch pad. She handed the sketch of The Tiger to Jesse, who stood nearby, watching the proceedings with quiet interest.

"I'll get this photocopied and pass it around the Central Asia section at the office." He slanted a quick look at Amanda, who looked ready to protest. "I will, of course, come up with a story that has nothing to do with you."

She subsided against the sofa cushions, remaining silent but still looking worried.

And tired. Stressed. The antibiotics had already wiped out her fever and were sending the infection into rapid decline. But the constant pressure on her must be exhausting.

What she needed—what they both needed—was a break. Get out of the self-imposed prison of Isabel's house and find a place where they could pretend the past two days had never happened.

A place like the hotel room on Rue du Miroir, where they

could escape into a world of their own creation. A world where they set the rules and drove the agenda.

And he knew just such a place.

"WHAT DO YOU THINK?" Rick waved his arm at the vista spread out in front of them, the smile in his voice barely audible over the roar of water.

Amanda slanted a look his way. He was grinning at her, looking rather pleased with himself. She bit back a grin of her own and pretended to be considering their surroundings with a critical eye. "Where are we, exactly?"

"We're exactly twenty yards from Crybaby Falls," he answered, reaching out his hand.

She took it and let him lead her forward until they reached the narrow wooden footbridge that crossed the wide, roiling stream just ten yards from the drop-off that formed the waterfall. The area was heavily forested on each side of the falls, the bridge the only sign of human habitation in view. Amanda was surprised to find no one else around, considering the beauty of the area. "Where are all the tourists?"

"It's Chickasaw County's little secret," he answered, bending close to her ear so he could lower his voice for effect. "The locals think this place is haunted and cursed, and they've conspired for over a century to keep outsiders from coming here and learning the secret of our shame."

She arched an eyebrow. "Or it's spring break, and all the tourists are in Florida working on an early tan?"

He laughed. "Or that."

He led her across the bridge and down a steep incline where nature had dug footholds in the craggy rock face. Halfway down the falls, the incline leveled off to a natural ledge, about ten feet square, where enterprising humans had stacked flat rock slabs to build a bench. Rick dusted off the bench and waved for her to sit.

"I thought you said you were taking me somewhere that would remind me of Tablis." She waved her hand at the woods surrounding the falls. "Nothing like this in Tablis."

"You're too literal," he scolded lightly, sitting next to her. "It's a little chilly—are you warm enough?"

She couldn't stop herself from snuggling closer to his warm side. "I'm fine."

He wrapped his arm around her shoulders, the touch casual. Friendly. But her body's response was anything but casual. Her entire nervous system seemed to hum with awareness of him. Of his warm male scent and the rasp of his unshaven jaw against her temple as he tucked her closer to ward off the cold.

He was trying to seduce her. He was being subtle about it, but she knew enough about men to know that he hadn't forgotten what he'd told her the night before.

He wanted her. He knew she wanted him.

It was just a matter of time before he tried to prove himself right. If she was going to keep her promise to herself to avoid any more messy complications in her life, she was going to have to make sure she won this battle of wills.

Unfortunately, sitting here cuddled up in the circle of his arms wasn't a very auspicious start for Team Amanda.

"There really is a ghost story connected to these falls," Rick said, his tone serious. "Two, actually. First, there was a Chickasaw woman stolen from her tribe by the Cherokees native to this part of Alabama. Betrothed to a young warrior of her own tribe who'd been killed by her captors, she gave birth to his son while in captivity. Soon after the baby's birth, a Cherokee tribesman planned to take her as his woman, but she was still grieving the father of her child. So she took her son and flung herself and the baby over the falls to their death."

Even though she knew the world was full of such legends,

almost entirely apocryphal, she couldn't hold back a shudder at the thought of the unhappy woman who saw so little hope in her future that she saw death as the better option.

She'd been so close to that point herself, near the end of her captivity and torture. If she hadn't made her escape from the makeshift prison, how much longer would she have lasted?

"But it's just a legend, of course," Rick murmured, tightening his arm around her shoulders. She looked up to find him watching her with worry in his eyes, looking as if he regretted ever bringing up the ghost story. "Most mothers who can't hack it leave their kids behind instead of jumping off a cliff with them."

She sensed a deeper story behind his words, but she didn't want to know it. The closer she let herself feel to him, the harder he'd be to resist. "What's the other ghost story?" she asked, as much to distract herself as him.

"That one, I'm sorry to say, is based in reality." Rick frowned. "Twenty years ago, a pregnant teenager plunged to her death over the falls. Everyone believes her lover killed her, though no one could ever prove it."

"How horrible."

"Folks around here swear that sometimes, at night, they can hear her calling her lover's name, as if she's pleading for mercy." Rick sighed. "Well. Not exactly the 'forget your problems' sort of mood I was trying to set."

"The world is full of dread as well as beauty," she said.

He rose to his feet and tugged at her hand. "Come on. It's too cold to be sitting out here."

With a groan, she joined him in the hike back to where they'd parked the car on the dirt road to the falls. A short drive later, down a winding dirt road littered with pine straw, they pulled up in front of a travel trailer parked at the edge of a large lake.

She cut her eyes at Rick. "Ta-da?"

He grinned at her. "It ain't the Ritz, but it's private and it's paid for."

The camper was a boxy metal monstrosity about twenty feet long and eight feet wide. But to her surprise, the interior of the camper seemed larger than the outside would have suggested, every bit of space maximized for comfort and function.

Rick dumped their bags on the brown sofa just inside the door. "I bought this a few months ago, after I started working for Jesse. If I was going to be this close to Gossamer Lake, I wanted to have a place by the water. And until I find time to pick out a plot of land and build myself a lake house, this will do."

He showed her the small kitchen and dining cubbyhole, then waved his hand at the queen-size bed snugged into the other end of the camper. "Sorry there's not any privacy—I bought it for overnight fishing trips and didn't go for the luxury model."

She lifted her gaze to his, not missing the feral gleam lurking behind his dark eyes. "And where are you going to sleep?" she asked flatly.

He bent and spoke in her ear, his breath hot against her cheek. "That, sugar, depends entirely on you." Drawing back, he flashed her a devilish smile and headed outside.

THEY SPENT THE REST of the afternoon fishing. "For dinner," Rick told her with a wry grin. "Or else it's peanut butter sandwiches for us tonight."

Fortunately, the small pier that jutted into Gossamer Lake near the camper seemed to be a haven for little black crappie, which snapped up the tiny chartreuse jigs as quickly as she and Rick flipped them in front of them. By the time the afternoon light began to wane, they'd caught twenty keeper-size sunfish, more than enough for dinner.

Rick cleaned and filleted the crappie, frying them in cornmeal on the small camper stove. Finding cans of vegetables in the tiny pantry, Amanda selected corn and turnip greens for their side dishes and heated them in the microwave next to the stove, adding spices from Rick's sparse collection.

Yet, despite the less-than-ideal cooking conditions she'd toiled under, Amanda found herself delighted with the results, finishing off two large fish fillets and extra servings of the vegetables. Only after she sat back against the banquette bench, wiping her hands on a paper napkin, did she realized Rick was watching her, a smile on his face.

"You must be feeling better. It's good to see you with a healthy appetite."

"Not sure how healthy it was," she said with a wry groan, patting her full stomach. "But it was good."

"How's your arm?"

She blinked with surprise at the question, realizing that she hadn't given her injury a second thought all day. "Better."

"We should change the dressing before bedtime."

"Okay. I'll do you if you'll do me." Before the words finished coming out of her mouth, she realized she'd made a big unforced error.

Rick grinned at her slip. The air between them supercharged in a second. "I've got no problem with that."

"You know what I meant."

"So, do you want me to do you first? Or should we save you for last?"

She got up from the banquette and carried her plate to the sink. "Stop it, Rick."

"Stop what?" His voice was right behind her, close

enough to stir the tendrils of hair that tickled her neck where they'd escaped her ponytail.

She turned to face him, her second mistake of the night. His eyes were midnight-dark, blazing with desire, and she felt as if the tiny room around them spun into nothingness, leaving only her and him and the fire licking between them, drawing her closer and closer, a moth seeking the flame.

"Do you remember that first night we met in Tablis?" he murmured, his fingers brushing her wrist on their way slowly up her arm. "You were wearing a dark blue dress cut up to—"

"I was on assignment," she breathed. "At a nightclub."

"Interesting how the CIA works—sending you to a nightclub when you're supposed to be tracking fundamentalist terrorists." His fingers had traveled all the way up to her collarbone, sprinkling goose bumps along the path he'd traced.

"You know the Kaziri terrorists used religion only as a tool. What they believed in was power." He had to stop doing whatever it was he was doing to her collarbone or she was going to melt into a puddle at his feet. "You were as likely to find them in a nightclub as in a mosque. They're notorious for liking blondes."

Rick looped a loose strand of her hair around his finger. "They're not alone."

She eased away from him before she lost all control. "I should go get the first-aid kit. You packed it, didn't you?"

"I'm going to take a shower first." He held her gaze for a long moment, a smile playing with his lips. Then he turned toward the small bathroom, stripping off his shirt as he went.

Amanda stared at the ripple of muscles in his retreating back, her heart pounding. She was still standing there, transfixed, when the shower came on.

Ah, hell, she thought, unzipping her jeans and letting

them fall to the floor. She walked out of her panties, shed her shirt and dropped her bra on the way to the bathroom.

Pushing aside the shower curtain just enough to step inside, she let her gaze move slowly up Rick's wet, naked body, her eyes locking finally with his. He arched one eyebrow at her, a slow grin curving his beautiful lips.

"You win," she said, and stepped into his arms.

RICK WOKE FROM A LIGHT DOZE at the sound of Amanda's voice purring, low and content, against his chest. "Where'd you find a candle in this place?" she asked.

He smiled, watching the warm golden light dancing around the camper ceiling. "I like to be prepared."

Her lips brushed his nipple, sending an electric shock straight to his core. "So, this is your designated love shack?"

"I meant prepared for power outages, sugar." He gave her bare backside a light slap, letting his hand linger on her thigh. "Although I also came prepared in other ways, as you well know."

Amanda snuggled closer, her breasts flattening against his ribs. "We never did get around to bandaging our wounds."

"And we really should do that," he murmured, running his hand over the curve of her bottom.

"If you don't stop that," she warned, squirming a little against his hand, "we won't."

With a sigh, he pulled his hand away and sat up, dragging her with him into a sitting position. "Let me take a look first." He'd helped her wash the wound while they were in the shower, and to his eyes, it seemed to have improved quite a bit. But just a day ago, she'd been quite ill from the infection, and the exertions of lovemaking, however pleasurable they may have been, might not have been good for her recovering body.

As he went to the kitchen for the first-aid kit, he gave himself a mental kick for not thinking about the effects on her. Time to start thinking with his head and not his—

"Guilt is not a good look on you." Amanda's voice was right behind him. He turned and found her standing there just a foot away, her bare skin glowing in the candlelight like burnished gold. She had lost weight since he'd last seen her in Tablis. Toughened, perhaps, her muscles more defined and her bones a little more visible beneath the flesh.

"You've been ill," he said. And he wasn't just talking about the past couple of days.

"I'm better," she said simply. She caught his hand in hers and tugged. "Come back to bed."

He followed her back to the bed and sat, handing over the first-aid kit when she held out her hand. She bandaged his wound first, making a soft murmur of sympathy when he winced at her ministrations.

"Sorry." She pressed a light kiss on the curve of his shoulder as she taped the bandage down.

Then it was his turn. He took care to give as little pain as possible as he smoothed ointment onto the wound and covered it with gauze. He kissed her shoulder, as well, but didn't stop there, tracing a path of nips and pecks lightly over the contours of her clavicle.

Dipping lower, he darted his tongue over her left nipple, making her gasp.

He sat back and shoved the supplies back into the first-aid kit, letting it drop over the side of the bed. Amanda laughed, reaching for him as he surged toward her, driving her back into the soft pillows.

He kissed her, a slow, deep, wet kiss, the kind they had rarely had time to share during their stolen moments in Kaziristan. She responded with a low groan, her hips pushing against his, telegraphing her impatience.

"Shh," he whispered against her lips, threading his fingers through hers and pinning her against the pillows. "We've got nowhere to go tonight. No need to hurry."

"If you go too slow, I'll explode," she warned, her eyes blazing blue fire.

He smiled down at her. "That could be fun, too."

She tugged her hands away from him and reached up to catch his face between her hands, pulling him down for a slow, sweet kiss. When he drew back to catch his breath, she gazed up at him, her blue eyes serious.

"I haven't been with anyone since we were together," she said in a hushed voice.

He cupped her face between his palms, touched by the admission. Seeing in her eyes that being with him meant something special to her, then as now.

"Neither have I," he admitted, kissing her.

They made love slowly, relearning each other with every touch, every kiss, every breathless word, until they rode a wave of pleasure into the heart of sweet madness.

The next coherent thought he had was that his ears were buzzing. It took a few seconds to realize that what he was hearing was actually his cell phone, vibrating quietly on the banquette table a few feet away.

He rolled away from Amanda, who grumbled as cool air filled the space between them. With irritation, he saw his brother Jesse's name on the display. "Yeah?"

"Where are you? I've been trying to reach you for hours."

"I'm at my trailer on the lake. Is something wrong?"

"Not wrong, exactly—" Jesse sounded hesitant.

"What is it?"

"There's a guy here, looking for Amanda."

Rick's chest tightened. "What?"

"He says it's urgent that he speaks with her." Jesse's voice lowered a notch. "He said Alexander Quinn sent him."

Chapter Thirteen

"I need to leave. Now." Amanda stuffed her supplies into the duffel bag at the foot of the bed in Isabel's guest room while Rick paced nearby, looking desperate.

"If Jesse thought you were in danger from this guy, he'd have told me." Rick caught her hand as she reached for the Smith & Wesson lying on the bed. "Are you just going to leave after what happened tonight?"

She tamped down the rush of emotions his words evoked and angled her chin at him like a weapon. "We had sex. It happens a million times a day all over the world. So what? It was great, really, but it's not worth dying for."

Amber fire danced in the depth of his dark eyes. "You are such a liar."

"You think sex is worth dying for?"

"I think what we could have together just might be worth dying for. If you'd give it a chance."

The sound of the front door opening stopped her from responding. She grabbed the Smith & Wesson and checked the clip, looking for somewhere in the small guest room to take cover. The bathroom was too small, giving her little room to maneuver and no place to hide. She eyed the window, wondering if she could get it open before whoever was walking down the hallway got to her.

"Stop it." Rick edged toward the door, keeping an eye on

her, as if he could read her intentions in her expression. “Let me see who it is.” He slipped out into the hallway.

She crossed quickly to the window and unlatched the lock. The window creaked a little as she pulled at it, but it wouldn’t give. Too much old paint—she’d have to get out her knife and see if she could pry the paint loose.

The door to the room opened again. Amanda swung her weapon to bear on the intruder.

It was Rick. He held up his hands, taking a quick step backward into the door.

She dropped the Smith & Wesson to her side, her heart racing, and let loose a quick profanity.

“He says his name is Damon North. And I believe he is who he says he is.” Rick took a slow, wary step toward her, one hand outstretched.

She crossed to him, pressing her forehead against his shoulder. He wrapped his arms around her and held her tightly for a long moment.

“Why do you believe him?”

“Because he brought someone to vouch for him.”

She looked up, intrigued.

“Remember the trouble my cousin and his wife had with MacLear SSU agents last year?” At her nod, he continued. “Well, Damon was working undercover as an SSU agent for Alexander Quinn. He helped Luke out, and Luke’s here to vouch for him.”

She arched her eyebrows in surprise. “CIA can’t do covert ops on American soil.”

“Damon wasn’t working for CIA. He was working for a private security company. But Quinn’s the one who gave him the tip about MacLear.”

She sighed. “And you trust your cousin?”

“Completely.”

Finally, she gave a nod. “Okay. I’ll hear what he has to

say." She tucked her pistol in the waistband of her jeans and nodded for Rick to open the door.

They found Jesse and two other men sitting in Isabel's living room. One of them was gray-eyed with dark hair cut high and tight. Former Marine, she thought instantly. The other man was black, handsome and powerfully built. His dark brown eyes followed her into the room with interest.

Isabel perched on the arm of the sofa next to her elder brother. She gave Amanda an encouraging smile.

Jesse stood. "Amanda, this is my cousin Luke Cooper and this—" he pointed to the black man "—is Damon North."

An alias, Amanda decided quickly. The kind of name a man would pick if he were creating a new identity.

North rose to his feet, greeting her with a nod. "Nice to finally meet you. Quinn's told me quite a bit about you."

Watching him through narrowed eyes, she answered him in a flat, no-nonsense tone. "If you knew a lot about me, you'd know better than to try to play me with a bunch of polite bull. What does Quinn want?"

"Your help," Damon answered just as flatly.

"Doing what?" Rick asked that question, edging closer to her as if to guard her flank.

"I'm sure you know by now that someone has put out a hit on you. From what we understand about what happened in Tennessee, at least one former MacLear Special Services Unit operative attempted to kill you."

"How do you know this?" Amanda asked.

"Because Alexander Quinn is who he is," Damon answered with a half smile. "You of all people should understand that."

She did. But knowing what kind of man Quinn was didn't make her feel any more charitable toward the old master spy or his cryptic, elliptical warnings. The man's entire being was built on secrets and lies. She wasn't sure anyone at the

CIA even knew the man's real name or where he came from. He seemed to have burst into the world, fully formed, twenty years ago, when he joined the CIA as an analyst. If he ever left the CIA, she suspected he would cease to exist, swallowed by the ether.

"Okay. What does Quinn want with me?"

"He didn't anticipate that you would run away."

"Was he the one who put the tracker in my tooth?"

Damon's surprise seemed genuine. "A tracker?"

Either Quinn didn't know—unlikely—or he hadn't told Damon about the GPS device. "Never mind. Either way, he tracked me down. I won't bother to ask how, because you'd never tell me."

"I can tell you," Jesse Cooper said. "I called a friend. Someone with a stake in Cooper Security."

Both Rick and Isabel turned to look at him, their expressions taut with surprise.

"Who?" Rick asked.

"I've been asked to keep his identity hidden," Jesse answered. "He has money, but he's not in a position to build a company using his own name and reputation."

Someone notorious? Amanda wondered. But before she could ask any more questions, Damon spoke again. He had a nice voice, low and cultured, but there was a sort of raw, feral power in his lean, muscular body and a fierce tension in his dark eyes that belied his outer veneer of sophistication. "It doesn't matter who Mr. Cooper called. The fact remains, Alexander Quinn learned of your location and sent me to help you."

She narrowed her eyes in disbelief. "Help me?"

"You're trying to find out why the former MacLear agents are hunting you. I can help you find out."

"Really? How?"

"Because I'm one of them."

Amanda's hand dropped to her waistband, her fingers closing over the grip of her Smith & Wesson.

"Hear him out," the Marine said.

"I'm not in the mood for more games."

"I'm not playing games," Damon insisted. "This is deadly serious. For the past three years, I've been undercover with the MacLear Special Services Unit. After MacLear collapsed a little over a year ago, I took care to maintain my cover. My involvement in the clash that led to the company's downfall was kept below the radar."

"By whom?" she asked.

"By me," Luke Cooper answered. "I kept Damon out of the mess so he could maintain his cover if needed."

Amanda felt Rick's hand flatten against her lower back, his touch warm and firm. She barely squelched the urge to lean back into his solid heat. "Okay. So, if you're one of the SSU bloodhounds on my scent, and you're working with Quinn, then you should know who hired your fellow goons to kill me." She quirked an eyebrow at Damon. "No offense."

He smiled slightly. "None taken. Unfortunately, I don't know who hired them. There's no band of brothers working in unison where the SSU is concerned. I wasn't included in this particular job, but I've been putting out feelers to some of the guys I knew, trying to get back into the fold."

"So you're not really one of them, then."

"I'm as close as you'll get, and I have the added benefit, to you, of not actually wanting you dead."

"Let's cut to the chase here," Rick said bluntly. "Why are you here and what do you want?"

"I have an idea how to smoke out the SSU agents who've taken the job of hunting you down," Damon told Amanda. "If we can get them to try an ambush, we can turn the tables on them."

"You're suggesting that Amanda offer herself up as bait."

Rick stepped around Amanda, putting himself between her and Damon. It was a touching show of chivalry, but Amanda wasn't the kind of woman who needed a man—or anyone else—to make her decisions and fight her battles for her.

She went around him and stepped closer to Damon. "What would the plan entail?"

Damon eyed both of them with wariness. "I have a contact from the SSU I've been cultivating ever since things fell apart. I was newer to the group than a lot of the guys, and I disappeared for a while right after the company crashed, so I'm still having to prove myself to some. But I think I can convince this guy that I can be of help to them. They know I did a lot of legwork in this area when I was assigned to go after Luke's wife and kid. I'm familiar with that side of the family, too—I know the players. I can give them information—inside information—they can't get anywhere else."

"They haven't connected me with Rick and his family," Amanda pointed out. "Or they'd already be here."

"Exactly. I can give them that detail. I can direct their attention here, where you and the Coopers will have home-field advantage in fighting back."

Amanda looked at the other Coopers gathered in the room—calm-eyed Jesse, who was watching the scene unfold as if he were an outside observer, and kindhearted Isabel, whose look of worry and sympathy touched a tender place Amanda didn't even know she possessed. The Marine, Luke Cooper, looked eager, as if he was itching to get another crack at the MacLear thugs.

Rick, however, was looking at her with gritty determination, poised to put an end to any more discussion of ambushes and playing bait.

"I have to think about it," she said aloud, even though her gut was telling her to say yes to Damon's suggestion. She wanted the danger over, even if it meant becoming a casualty in whatever proxy war the former SSU agents were fighting.

She was tired of the limbo in which she'd been living for the past three years.

But making a rash move was never a good idea. Good soldiers planned ahead, even if the plans never survived the first clash. Preparation was as much mental as physical, and she needed to think. To figure out what she really wanted and her best hope of getting it. She needed to be alone, to shut out the noise and chaos for just a little while.

"How can I get in touch with you?" she asked Damon.

"I'll call. Will you have an answer tomorrow afternoon?"

She nodded. She had an answer now, really. She just had to run through all the possible outcomes before she could commit to such a dangerous plan.

And she had to figure out what to do about Rick.

He wouldn't let her go through with playing bait. Not without a fight. And if she decided to go through with Damon's plan, then time for them had grown very short indeed.

She didn't want to spend what might be her last few hours with Rick embroiled in an argument.

On his way out, Damon stopped and shook Amanda's hand. "I'll talk to you soon."

He let go of her hand, leaving something behind. As Rick went with the others to walk Damon out, Amanda uncurled her hand to find a small slip of paper with a phone number on it.

She pushed it into the pocket of her jeans as Isabel and Rick returned. Everyone else had left with Damon.

"I'm going to head to bed. I have a long day tomorrow.' Isabel retreated to her bedroom, leaving Rick and Amanda alone in the living room.

Rick caught her face between his palms, making her look up at him. "You can't do this."

She curled her hands around his wrists. "I don't want to talk about this right now."

"Okay." He brushed his lips against hers, the kiss so sweet and undemanding it threatened to bring tears to her eyes.

She fought them off, forcing herself to step back from his embrace and find her own feet. "Do you mind if I have a little time alone? I have so much to think about—"

"I'll be here if you need me." He gestured at the sofa.

"No, I don't want you to stay on the sofa."

"You want me to go home?"

She shook her head. "I want you to stay with me tonight. Just to sleep," she added when she caught a flicker of heat in his eyes. "I'd feel weird with Isabel in the next room."

He smiled. "You're asking a lot."

"I know. But you're man enough to handle it, aren't you?"

"I guess we'll see." He tucked a strand of hair behind her ear. "How long do you need to be alone?"

"Half hour? I just need some peace and quiet to think. You're used to being surrounded with family, but it's new to me." She caught his hand, gave it a squeeze. "Thank you for today. For the trip to the lake and for—"

"The mind-blowing sex?" he supplied with a wicked smile.

"Yeah. For that, too."

"Oh, believe me, it was my pleasure." He kissed her again, and this time, there was nothing sweet or undemanding about it. She felt heat pour through her like lava, spreading inexorably to every atom of her body. When he pulled away, she felt unsteady on her feet, as if his kiss were a potent drug.

"I'm going to take a quick turn outside the house to make sure everything's secure, then I'll lock up for the night."

"Okay." She turned toward the guest room, surprised by her body's reluctance to move away from him. Even in

Tablis, at the height of their passionate affair, she'd never had trouble walking away.

Maybe that's because she'd believed, even the day they ended their relationship, that it wasn't really over.

But now, with a death sentence hanging over her head and no sure way out of the trouble she was in, each time she walked away from Rick felt as if it could be the last.

THE PERIMETER WAS SECURE, the doors and windows safely locked. Shutting off the lights, he went quietly into the guest room, in case Amanda had already fallen asleep. The light was off, so he undressed in the dark, stripping to his boxers and a T-shirt, and eased under the covers next to her.

"I'm awake," she said softly, turning her head to look at him in the dark. Only a faint moon glow through the window shed any light at all, edging her silhouette in pale blue.

He scooted closer under the covers, wrapping his arms around her and spooning her from behind. "Oh, you're warm."

"And your hands are like ice," she whispered, plucking them away when he slipped his fingers under the hem of her short cotton T-shirt. "Is it that cold outside?"

"Yeah, but it's supposed to warm up tomorrow."

"Good. I'm tired of being cold."

He waited for her to settle back against him before he spoke again. "I don't want you to be Alexander Quinn's bait."

"I don't want to talk about that now."

"You never want to talk about anything." He tried not to let the full force of his frustration tint the tone of his voice, but he didn't succeed.

She caught one of his hands and brought it to her mouth,

pressing a kiss against his knuckles. "In Tablis, we had other things to do besides talk."

"Yeah, well, you took that off the table tonight."

She laughed softly. "Touché."

"And this isn't Tablis, anyway. I like to think we're a little past the point of living only for the moment."

"Maybe *you* are."

"And you're not?"

She turned over to face him. "Our timing stinks."

He stroked the hair falling across her cheek. "I can wait for things to settle down. I'm not going anywhere."

Threading her fingers with his, she nuzzled her nose against his chin. "You're different now, you know."

"I'm older. More patient."

"And more challenging."

"Is that good?" he asked, hoping she'd say yes.

She seemed to consider the question for a moment, long enough to make him worry. "Yeah," she said finally. "It's good. I've been thinking a lot about what I want my life to be, now that I'm not a spy anymore, and I don't think the things that made me content before can ever make me content again."

He couldn't stop himself from asking, "Including me?"

She touched his lips with her fingertip. "You're not the same as you were before, remember? So you don't count." Her voice took on a teasing tone. "You get a fresh start to prove yourself, Cooper."

"But you won't let me," he said in an equally light tone, sneaking his hand up to brush lightly against the curve of her breast. "For instance, I could prove how quiet I can be—"

"I'm not sure I could be," she moaned, arching her back as his thumb brushed over her hardening nipple.

He knew an opening when he saw one. Dipping his head,

he covered her nipple with his mouth, tonguing the hard nub through the thin cotton of her T-shirt. She dug her fingers into his back, her thighs parting to accept the pressure of his hips against hers.

They made love quietly but frantically, as if they could erase the years apart with sheer determination. And for a moment, as she surged in his arms, drawing him with her into a maelstrom of pleasure, he thought they'd succeeded.

But afterward, lying with Amanda's body draped over his in contented slumber, Rick couldn't shake the feeling that no matter how they tried, some nightmares could never be erased.

And something dangerous was on its way.

Chapter Fourteen

"You don't have to do it." Rick's voice rumbled in Amanda's ear, seductive despite the topic of conversation. She shouldn't have let him coax her into a picnic down by the creek below Isabel's house. He had immediately taken advantage of their time alone to begin a slow-burning seduction.

She knew his show of passion wasn't entirely agenda-free. He wanted her to say no to Damon North's request, and he wasn't above using sex to get his way.

She kind of liked that about him. But it didn't change a thing. She'd made her decision last night, lying in Rick's arms in the drowsy aftermath of lovemaking. As long as there were MacLear agents out there, gunning for her for reasons she couldn't fathom, she'd always be running.

She didn't know if she and Rick had what it took to be together long-term. She wasn't even sure she wanted to be with *anyone* long-term.

But she was tired of running.

She turned her head to press her lips against the underside of his jaw, enjoying the low groan that escaped his throat. "Isabel's at work. The house is empty—"

He dipped his head and kissed her, a light, nipping touch of his mouth against hers. "Or we could stay out here and hash this thing out."

With a sigh, she pulled away from him, tucking her knees up to her chest. His hand stroked lightly down her back, the touch comforting and undemanding.

"You've already decided you want to do it, haven't you?"

She nodded. "I need to know who's behind this mess and why. Don't you?"

"Of course. But that doesn't mean you have to put your neck on the chopping block. We've barely started looking into who The Tiger might be—"

"And he might have nothing to do with this at all," Amanda countered, turning to look at him. "And there's something else we have to consider—the CIA knows about you and me."

He arched an eyebrow. "I'm not sure—"

"Before, I mean. In Kaziristan. The agency knew I was involved with you."

He looked surprised. "You said it was just Quinn."

"I thought it was, until I was debriefed after my escape from al Adar. For a while, they thought you might have been involved in my abduction—that you'd tipped off al Adar about where to find me."

He looked horrified. "My God."

She lifted her hand to his face, running her fingers lightly over the cleft in his chin. "I told them you had nothing to do with it. I convinced them."

"I would never—"

She turned her body to face him, twining her hands with his. "I know. But the CIA knew about us. And that tracker in my tooth means something. The MacLear team lost our scent after we got rid of the tracker. What if someone at the CIA *is* working with the SSU? What if there's a mole?"

"Why aren't they here already?"

She felt a flutter of pain in the center of her chest. "I also convinced them that our breakup had been bitter and irrevocable. I told them you'd taken up with another woman and that I never wanted to see you again."

He stared at her, comprehension dawning in his eyes. He lifted one big hand to her face, cupping her cheek with heartbreaking tenderness. "To protect me?"

There wasn't much point in pretending otherwise. "I knew what kind of hell they could have given you if I didn't get them off your trail. I didn't want that for you."

He leaned in and kissed her, tenderness infusing the caress until she had to pull back to keep herself from breaking into tears. As she struggled for control, he gave her room.

When she felt steadier, she started gathering the remains of their picnic lunch. He pitched in, helping her wrap up the leftovers and put them back in the basket.

"I have to go into the office for a little while," he told her as he stood and reached down his hand to help her to her feet. "There are some calls I need to make."

"Go ahead. I'll take care of this," she said with a swing of the picnic basket. She shot him a wicked smile. "I could use a nap after last night, anyway."

Smiling, he bent and kissed her, slow and deep. For a moment, every thought in her head seemed to flee in the face of the fire rushing through her at his touch.

His tongue tangled with hers, branding her with heat. Pulling away with reluctance, he gazed at her with passion-drunk eyes. "I'll be back in a couple of hours. Should I send Isabel back to stay with you?"

"I'm capable of protecting myself now," she said firmly, walking with him to his car. "I haven't run a fever in twenty-four hours, and I can barely feel any pain in my arm anymore. Plus, I'm armed and dangerous."

He smiled at her confidence, though his eyes were deadly

serious. "You get out of here if you feel the least bit threatened."

He'd shown her a hidden door in the laundry room that led to a storm cellar behind the house. If someone tried to invade the house, she could escape through the cellar door, which was camouflaged by a toolshed in Isabel's backyard.

"I will," she promised. "And thank you."

He gave her a quizzical look. "For what?"

"For lunch," she answered.

For giving her something to fight for again.

He stroked her cheek. "My pleasure."

She watched him drive away, waiting until he was safely out of sight to pull the slip of paper Damon had given her from the pocket of her jeans. She walked back into Isabel's house and into the guest room, pulling her duffel bag from where it lay on the floor by the bed. Inside one of the inner pockets she found the small prepaid cell phone she'd bought a couple of months ago.

She'd had a scare when she ran into a tourist who looked just like a woman she'd worked with at the U.S. embassy in Tablis. It hadn't been her colleague, as it turned out, but the close call had been enough to make her add a few essentials to her disaster kit, including a prepaid phone she could use in a pinch without signing up for a contract.

She'd charged the battery a couple of days before she'd gotten Quinn's package. To her relief, there was still plenty of battery power left to make the call.

Taking a deep breath, she dialed the number Damon had given her, waiting for him to answer.

But it wasn't Damon's voice on the other line.

"Hello, Audrey," said Alexander Quinn.

WHEN HE ARRIVED AT Cooper Security, Rick went straight to his brother's office, entering without bothering to knock.

Jesse looked up, his expression tight with annoyance. "The door was closed for a reason."

"Who'd you call?"

Jesse didn't pretend he didn't know what Rick was asking. "I told you last night, I agreed to keep his identity secret."

Rick slapped his hand hard on Jesse's desk. "I let you in on what was going on with Amanda. I convinced her she could trust you. And you were keeping secrets all along."

"Not secrets that could hurt her."

"How the hell am I supposed to know that?"

Jesse rose and faced him across the desk, his nostrils flaring with anger. "Because I'm your brother and I wouldn't do anything to hurt you. Or someone you cared about."

"So prove it. Tell me who's bankrolling this place."

Jesse's eyes narrowed.

"You think I didn't know that your Marine Corps pension couldn't lease a room in this office building, much less the whole damned thing?" Rick laughed. "I'm not stupid, no matter what you think of my life choices."

"I don't think you're stupid." Jesse sank into his chair, looking up at Rick with a frown. "I worried about MacLear, that's all. I'd heard things—"

"And I didn't listen." Rick settled in the chair across from his brother. "You were right."

Jesse was silent a moment, his gaze seeming to pierce all the way through Rick.

Rick held his tongue, realizing his brother was trying to make a decision. Silence was his best hope, since anything he said these days seemed destined to make his brother angry.

"His name is Maddox Heller."

Rick gave a start. "Mad Dog Heller?"

Jesse nodded.

Rick sat back, surprised. Maddox Heller had been a

Marine Corps security guard working at the U.S. embassy in Tablis, Kaziristan, during the embassy siege a few years earlier. After the brutal near-decapitation of a female interpreter by al Adar rebels trying to lure out Maddox and the embassy personnel he was guarding, the State Department had seized on Heller's inaction to make him the public face of all that had gone wrong at the embassy that day.

The innuendos had been entirely unfair, but the State Department officials—including Barton Reid—had made sure only their side of the story was told.

The last Rick had heard, Maddox Heller was living somewhere in the Caribbean, out of the public eye. "Where the hell did a disgraced Marine get enough money to open a shop like this?"

"He wasn't disgraced," Jesse snapped. "He was railroaded."

"I know that. But about the money?"

"An inheritance," Jesse answered. "He wanted to use the money for something worthwhile, but he knew that putting his name on an agency wouldn't be great for business."

"So you're his shell company?"

Jesse shot his brother a wry grin. "Not entirely. I have a stake in this place, too. I believe in what we're doing here. Don't you?"

"Of course." Rick knew that Cooper Security was doing more than just pulling in fees. The money they got from their big jobs helped pay for some pro bono and low-fee jobs they did for ordinary people who'd found themselves pitted against powerful bad actors both here in the U.S. and in places abroad. "How does Heller have access to Alexander Quinn?"

"Maybe you should ask him yourself," Jesse said, smiling a little as Rick shot him a questioning look. "That's what you really came here for, right? You want to talk to Heller yourself, to find out what he thinks Quinn's really up to."

"Yes," Rick admitted. "Can you put me in touch with him?"

"I can find out if he'll see you."

"See me? I don't have time for a trip to the Caribbean."

Jesse's smile widened. "You don't have to. Heller lives about twenty minutes away in Borland."

"ARE YOU GOING TO QUIT playing games and just tell me what the hell's going on?" Amanda's nerves had gone way past the edge and headlong into primal-scream territory within a minute of double-talk on the phone with Alexander Quinn.

"Someone's put out a hit on you," Quinn answered flatly.

"Tell me something I don't know."

"I think it's connected to your captivity in Kaziristan."

"You think?"

Quinn didn't answer, adding to Amanda's growing conviction that she was up against a double agent. And Quinn knew it.

"You think someone at CIA is dirty."

"I know a lot of people at CIA are dirty." Quinn's voice held a hint of humor. "It's part of our job description."

"I'm talking about a traitor."

"I know." Quinn grew serious. "And you've always had good instincts."

"Do you know who?"

"If I did, he'd be dead." Quinn's cold tone sent a shiver down Amanda's spine.

"How does MacLear play into this?"

"Surely you've figured that out."

"SSU hasn't entirely disbanded."

"No, it hasn't. And they're selling themselves out to the highest bidder." Quinn sounded bemused. "I always figured them for cockroaches, but I had no idea just how indestructible they'd turn out to be."

Which fit Damon's story about how he'd come to work for SSU—Quinn had sent him to infiltrate the secret security force and bring the company down from the inside. "Why do you think the hit on me has something to do with Kaziristan?"

"Haven't you wondered why I wasn't the one to debrief you after you escaped?"

"Yes," she admitted. "They said you were on assignment."

"They *sent* me on assignment." His voice dropped an octave. "I should've been there. You needed me, and they kept me away from you. I've spent three years trying to figure out why."

"And what have you concluded?" she asked, her voice strained by a terrible thought racing through her brain.

Quinn voiced her thought for her. "I think someone big at the CIA knew who took you and didn't want you to tell what you knew to anyone who could put a kink in his plans."

She closed her eyes, feeling sick. "Quinn, I don't know the name of the man who debriefed me. He never told me, and I never asked. I'd never seen him before—"

"He may not have been CIA at all," Quinn murmured. "He may have been contracted by whoever wanted to hide your captors' identities."

"But Mitch Jefferson okayed the interrogation."

"Jefferson left the CIA last year. Took early retirement." Quinn's voice darkened. "Now I'm wondering if that's just a coincidence."

Amanda passed a hand over her burning eyes. "I don't want to believe it. Jefferson seemed like one of the good ones."

"He could have been a dupe. If the order came from high enough up—"

"How high up?" she asked, appalled.

"Very. Too high for me to reach, which is why I'm bypassing the CIA altogether." He sounded impatient. "Listen, I can't stay on this line much longer. You do what Damon asks. Okay? I wouldn't ask it of you if I thought there was a better way. You're running out of time, and all those bastards need is to get lucky just once."

"I'll do it," she agreed. She'd already decided she would.

"Go answer the door." He hung up the phone.

She stared at the phone for a second. Then a soft rapping sound at the front of the house set her nerves jangling.

She did as Quinn asked, opening the door to Damon North. He stood in the doorway, holding a large canvas bag. "You talk to Quinn?"

"Yes."

"Then let's get ready to go."

Her eyes widened. "Now?"

"If you stick around, Cooper will come back and try to talk you out of it." Damon motioned for her to let him in the house. "You know you've got to do this."

"Don't you have to set something up?" she asked as they went back to the guest room to gather her gear.

"Already done." He set his bag on her bed, unzipped it and pulled out a camouflage coverall. "Here, wear this."

She looked up from her duffel bag, her hand still on the butt of the SIG Sauer she'd selected from her small collection. "You and Quinn were pretty confident I'd lay my neck on the line for you, huh?"

"You're not doing this for us. You're doing it for yourself. You're the target. We figured you couldn't give up the chance to finally stop running away."

She looked down at the pistol in her hand. It was sleek, black and deadly. But it might not prove to be much protection against a small army of ruthless, well-trained men on a mission.

Running away didn't seem like such a bad option.

But once a person started running, it was next to impossible to stop. Sooner or later, you had to turn around, plant your feet and make a stand. Might as well make hers while she was still in fighting condition.

"Okay," she said, pulling ammunition from the bag and grabbing the compact Walther she liked to carry in an ankle holster as a backup weapon. She belted the holster around her ankle and rose to face Damon, who was holding the coverall open for her. She stepped into the legs and zipped up the front. "I need somewhere to put my holster."

Damon pulled a camouflage belt out of the bag. She belted it around her waist and clipped her holster to the belt, then went across the room to the desk by the window.

"What are you doing?" Damon asked as she scrabbled through the drawers.

"I need to leave Rick a note."

Damon shook his head. "He'll come after you."

"He'll come after me if I leave here without a note." She found a small notepad and a pen in one of the drawers and jotted a quick note. "I'm telling him I'm going for a long walk and not to expect me back until four." Rick said he'd be gone a couple of hours, which meant he'd be back around three. She'd get a three-hour head start before he started looking.

If she was lucky, it would all be over by then.

One way or another.

Chapter Fifteen

Maddox Heller's place in Borland, Alabama, a town about twenty minutes from Maybridge, seemed pretty ordinary at first glance. Nestled at the end of a winding, wooded road, the two-story farmhouse sat on a small clearing about thirty yards back from the road. The front yard was mostly wooded, shaded by towering pines, while behind the house, a natural garden spread out, inviting and abloom with daffodils, hyacinths and tulips.

Rick parked in an empty place in the driveway and walked up the flagstone walkway to the front door, wondering what he'd find inside. Rick had never met Maddox Heller, but the former Marine had been notorious for a while a few years back, shortly after the embassy siege that had led to the long period of instability in Kaziristan.

As the State Department's chosen whipping boy, Heller had faced a dishonorable discharge and plenty of blame from the media and politicians eager to deflect attention from their own slow reactions to intelligence-agency warnings of impending unrest in Kaziristan.

Then another crisis came along, the news cycle rolled on and Heller had disappeared from the headlines.

Rick knew him only by the newspaper photos he'd seen and the still shots cable news and broadcast stations had put on-screen while sensationalizing his story. He expected to find a slightly older version of the Marine Heller had been when the story erupted.

Instead, he found a cheerful-looking man with sandy hair worn a little long and at least two days' growth of beard on his smiling face. He wore jeans and a long-sleeve T-shirt stained with the same grape jelly currently covering the sticky fingers of a dark-haired toddler perched on his hip.

"Sorry about the mess—Daisy's going through the terrible twos." Heller started to reach out his hand to shake Rick's, spotted the jelly goo on his palm and drew back with an apologetic smile. "Iris will be here to take her off our hands in a second—she's on her way home from the nursery."

"If this is a bad time—"

"No, come on in." Heller had a strong Southern drawl, far stronger than his own, which so much time out of Alabama had muted and tempered. "Daisy Mae, your mama's gonna have to give you a bath in the middle of the day. What do you say to that?"

"Baf!" Daisy patted her father's face with delight, leaving grape-jelly stains on his cheeks.

"You got any kids?" Heller asked as he led Rick into a comfortable, lived-in den. He grabbed a large pink diaper bag off the sofa cushion and dug inside, still gripping his daughter on his hip. He pulled out a small, flat box and handed it to Rick. "Can you open that and give me a wipe?"

Rick complied, answering Heller's earlier question as he handed over the wet wipe. "No kids," he answered, thinking of Amanda. She seemed about the least likely candidate for motherhood he knew, and given his experience with his own mother, who hadn't been able to take motherhood or marriage to a small-town cop, he wasn't going to force any woman into a life she couldn't handle. "Don't think it's in the cards for me."

Heller took the wipe and went to work on the toddler's sticky hands and face. The little girl struggled to keep away from the wipe, making a game of it. "I'd have said the same thing a few years ago. Until Iris came along."

"Who made the mess in the kitchen?" A woman's voice floated in from somewhere near the back of the house, making both Heller and the baby turn in that direction, grins on their faces. A moment later, a slim, pretty woman with dark, wavy hair and bright brown eyes entered the room, her eyes alight at the sight of her family. "I see it was a peanut butter and jelly day!" She held out her arms and the toddler wriggled against her father's grasp until he set her down. She raced to her mother on plump, churning legs.

The woman picked up the little girl and gave her a big kiss. "Sorry I'm a little late—Lily dropped by with Casey and Seth—" She stopped short, realizing there was someone else in the room. "Oh, hi. You must be Rick. I'm Iris Heller."

"I told her we were expecting you," Heller explained.

"I'll just take Daisy to the bathroom to wash up and then we'll go outside and play before it starts getting colder." Iris gave her husband a quick kiss and headed down the hallway, out of sight.

"I didn't know someone else would be here."

"Iris knows everything I know at this point, and I assume you're here to find out what I know, right?"

"Right."

"So let's get started." Heller wiped his hands and face with the wet wipe and tossed it in a nearby trash can. "Jesse faxed me over the sketch of the man who tortured your friend. I've got to say, I was a little surprised by it."

"Why?"

Heller picked up a folder sitting on a nearby desk and opened it, pulling out a fax copy of the sketch. "I think I know this guy. He was a little younger when I knew him, and his hair is longer in this picture, but I'd just about swear it's a guy I knew named Khalid Mazir."

Something about the name seemed familiar, but Rick couldn't place it. "And why's that surprising?"

"Because the Khalid Mazir I knew was a bright, Westernized kid. His daddy was the deputy minister of finance for the regime in place when al Adar took the embassy under siege. Old Zoli Mazir ended up gettin' killed a couple of weeks later in a car bombing outside the ministry building."

Rick had to admit, Khalid Mazir didn't sound like a likely suspect for an al Adar operative. "Maybe Khalid just looks like this guy."

"Except for this birthmark." Heller pointed to a kidney-shaped dark mark just under the left eye of the man in the sketch. "Khalid Mazir definitely had this same birthmark."

"So maybe the kid radicalized after his father's death."

"Or before," Heller said bleakly.

"So, is it just me, or does it still seem pretty unlikely that Khalid Mazir would bother putting out a hit on a woman he tortured three years ago?"

"Actually," Heller said, "I'd say it's pretty damn likely, when you consider what the man is doing these days."

"Which is what?"

Heller met Rick's gaze, his slate-blue eyes dark with concern. "Running for president of Kaziristan."

"I CONTACTED SALVATORE BECKETT and told him I knew where to find you." Damon North drove up the winding mountain road, taking the turns at scary speeds.

Amanda clutched the dashboard and held on, her heart thudding wildly in her chest. "How's this going to work? Is Quinn sending backup for us?"

Damon darted a glance her way but didn't answer.

Her stomach dipped. "Tell me we're not up against an army of mercs alone."

"We can't drag an army of our own into the woods. They'll see us coming and all hell will break loose."

"We're supposed to take on the whole crew ourselves?"

"Sort of."

"Stop the car."

He looked over at her. "Don't be stupid."

"You're talking about a suicide mission—but I'm guessing you're not the one who'll be in the crosshairs, am I right?"

"I'm not going to put you anywhere near the crosshairs." Damon sounded sincere, but Amanda's trust was stretched past the breaking point.

"Just tell me what you're planning."

"I need you to back me up."

She frowned. "I don't understand."

"I'm going to meet them. I'm going to tell them that the Coopers double-crossed me and that they've hidden you away somewhere. I'm going to convince them that I'm the only chance they have of finding you."

"This isn't about getting them off my back at all, is it?" She stared at him in disbelief. "This is about getting you back in with MacLear."

"Not for real. This is about finishing the job Quinn and I started a few years ago."

"How the hell am I supposed to know what's real or not?" She shook her head, furious at herself for putting herself in such a dangerous position.

"Didn't Quinn tell you to go with me?"

"Yes, but I don't know what his agenda is. He's a professional liar, and he's put agents in the line of fire before if he thought the risk was worth it."

"Just please—trust me. It's important that we don't take

this group down yet. There's someone bigger involved. Quinn and I are both convinced of it, especially the way things are going in the Barton Reid investigation. Someone's pulling strings, and we're about to lose everything we've worked for."

Amanda's lips thinned with annoyance. "Not my problem."

"Damned well *is* your problem. As long as the SSU operatives are still out there, gunning for hire, then people like you will always be in the line of fire. Quinn told me you weren't the kind of agent who worried only about her own skin."

"I'm not an agent anymore," she said blackly. "And I have other people to worry about."

"Yeah, well, this way, you're keeping the Coopers out of the battle zone. Isn't that what you want?"

It was—of course it was. And there was a part of her that knew Damon was right—catching a small portion of the mercenaries today wasn't nearly as valuable as infiltrating the whole group and strategically weakening them from the inside out so that the whole group might one day topple all at once.

But Damon's plan wouldn't do a damn thing to end the limbo her own life was in at the moment.

In the back of her head, she heard Alexander Quinn's voice, low and intense. *Do the job. Everything else is secondary.*

She just wasn't sure she believed that anymore.

RICK TRIED CALLING ISABEL'S house from his car, but nobody answered. He had ID blocking on his cell phone, which would prevent Amanda from being able to tell who was calling, even if she knew his number. He wasn't really surprised that she let the call go to voice mail.

He called Jesse and caught him up on what he'd learned from Maddox Heller. "He seems pretty sure that the man in the sketch is Mazir. Which could definitely explain why there's a hit squad after her."

Jesse spat out a profanity that made Rick's eyebrows arch. His brother was usually unflappable. "From what I've read, Mazir is running as a democratic reformer."

"I seem to recall a few dictators who claimed to be representing the people before they rose to power and showed their real faces," Rick growled. "If Amanda were to tell the press what Mazir did to her, the kind of torture and treachery he's capable of—"

"Whatever he's planning for Kaziristan would be in jeopardy," Jesse finished for him, his voice grim.

"Exactly. I'm heading to Isabel's—"

"I'll meet you there." Jesse hung up.

Jesse wasn't the only Cooper at Isabel's house when Rick arrived. The whole gang was there, and they didn't look happy.

"Where's Amanda?" he asked as he looked around Isabel's living room and didn't see her.

"We're not sure," Isabel answered. She was sitting at the small desk in the living room, her laptop computer open in front of her. "I checked the bedroom when I got here about ten minutes ago and found a note from her saying she went for a walk by the creek. But I've been up and down the creek and didn't see any sign of her. Not even footprints."

"But we did find tire tracks in the dirt at the edge of the driveway." Wade pulled out his cell phone and showed Rick an image on the small display screen. "They don't match any of our vehicles. But we think it may match Damon North's vehicle."

"And you said the surveillance cameras on the visitor parking lot were too intrusive," Jesse said to Rick, his smile grim. “I’ve got Branson in security pulling the surveillance shots of North’s vehicle. He’ll be emailing them to Isabel any minute.”

“I’ve already emailed her this picture for comparison,” Wade said. “If we have a good shot of the tire treads, we should be able to figure out if it’s Damon’s Subaru.”

“Email’s here,” Isabel said. “Let’s see what we’ve got.”

They crowded around the laptop as Isabel brought up the images on the email from the office. There were three shots from different angles. The third shot, taken from almost eye level, seemed the best chance of getting a good look at the tires. Isabel increased the image size, and the distinctive crosshatch tread came into view.

She pulled up the track Wade had shot with his phone.

“Same tread,” Shannon murmured, looking at Rick.

The rest of his siblings turned to look at him, as well.

An ache started forming deep in his gut. “Maybe he made the track when you brought him by here last night.”

Jesse shook his head. “I drove. The Subaru stayed parked at the office.”

“I think we need to conclude she’s with Damon,” Megan said. “The question is, did she go willingly?”

“Where’s the note she left?” Rick asked Isabel.

“Over here.” Shannon crossed to the coffee table and picked up a folded sheet of paper. She handed it to Rick.

He read over the simple note. *Cabin fever setting in. Taking a walk by the creek. Don’t worry, I’m armed.* She had signed it with her initial.

“She went willingly,” he said aloud.

“How do you know?” Shannon asked.

“She signed the note with her initial. We had a signal, back in Kaziristan, when we were seeing each other. Amanda and I agreed that if something happened to one of us and we had a chance to leave a note, the signal that we were in danger would be signing our full names. If everything was fine, we'd sign with the initial. She wants me to think everything's fine."

"Which means Damon convinced her it would be better for her to go alone, without your interference." Megan stepped closer, putting her hand on his shoulder. "She knew you didn't want her to put her neck on the chopping block."

"She should have trusted me."

Isabel turned away from the laptop. "She didn't want to argue and she didn't want to see you get hurt."

"She didn't have the right to make that choice for me."

"And you didn't have the right to tell her she couldn't put her life on the line for something she thought was worth doing."

Rick narrowed his eyes, wondering how much of his sister's passionate defense of Amanda's choice was wrapped up in her own issues regarding her partner's death. According to Isabel, Scanlon had deliberately left her in the dark about the call he'd received luring him to a warehouse in Virginia that, it turned out, had been rigged to explode.

Telling her that Scanlon had saved her life by leaving her out of the investigation didn't seem to appease Isabel's feelings of betrayal any more than telling him that Amanda was trying to protect him made him feel any better about her decision to go with Damon by herself.

"Where would he take her?" he asked. "What's his agenda?"

"The plan was to use her for bait." Megan turned to Jesse. "Did Damon tell you anything about his plan?"

Jesse shook his head. "I thought he'd discuss the details once Amanda decided what she wanted to do, and I didn't want to spook him by asking too many probing questions."

Rick looked at his brother. Since when did Jesse have a problem asking probing questions?

"I'm not keeping any secrets here," Jesse said.

"That's new," Rick shot back.

"Enough, already!" Megan stepped into the space between them. "Why don't we table the family squabble until we find Amanda and make sure she's safe?"

"How are we going to do that?" Shannon asked. "We don't know where he'd have taken her." She looked at Rick. "Does she have a cell phone?"

"I don't know," he admitted. "If she does, I don't have the number. Have any of you looked through her things?"

"No—we thought we'd wait and see if you knew where she might be," Shannon answered.

He moved past them and entered the guest room, stopping inside the door to look around. Closing his eyes, he tried to remember how they'd left the room. They'd slept late, not getting up until Isabel had already left for work. Amanda had taken care to remake the bed that morning after they rose, putting the used sheets in the laundry.

Her duffel bag was on the floor where she'd left it. He unzipped the canvas bag and looked around the interior. He knew she'd had three weapons—a Walther, a Smith & Wesson and a SIG Sauer. The Smith & Wesson was still there. The other two pistols were gone. So were at least three boxes of ammunition. She was armed, at least.

Near the bottom of the duffel bag, he found a small slip of paper, wrinkled from where it had been folded into a small square. On the paper was a phone number, written in bold, masculine strokes. Rick pulled his cell phone from his pocket and dialed the number.

A man's voice answered. A familiar voice. "Pizza City. Takeout or delivery?"

Gripping the phone more tightly, Rick swallowed a profanity.

It was Alexander Quinn.

Chapter Sixteen

"Where's Amanda, Quinn?" Rick growled into the phone.

Quinn's calm voice answered, "Don't interfere, Cooper."

Anger rose in Rick's chest. "Is she in danger?"

"Of course. But she's trained to handle danger."

"She's with Damon North?"

Quinn didn't answer.

"I know she is. What is he planning to do?"

"He's not really using her as bait. He just needs her with him as backup in case things go wrong."

Rick couldn't tell if Quinn was telling the truth or not. A liar that accomplished was hard enough to read face-to-face. Over the phone, Rick didn't have a chance in hell of seeing through the subterfuge.

"If something happens to her, Quinn, I will hunt you down and kill you myself."

"Or die trying."

"If that's what it takes."

The line went dead on Quinn's end of the call. Rick slapped his phone shut, uttering a low profanity.

"Who was on the phone?" Jesse's voice behind him made him jerk with surprise. He turned and found his brother in the open doorway, his arms folded and his eyes watchful.

"Alexander Quinn. His phone number was in the bottom of her bag. I think she's been in contact with him."

"Did he tell you anything?"

"Only that Damon North doesn't actually intend to use her as bait."

"What does that mean?"

"I don't know." Rick raked his hands through his hair, feeling stymied. "If he's not using her for bait, what's he using her for? Quinn says it's for backup, but I don't see how that makes any sense at all."

Megan stuck her head through the door, pushing Jesse aside. "I just called Aaron—reported an abduction so the sheriff's department can set up roadblocks. It may not keep them from getting out of the county, but it'll make it harder. Meanwhile, we can cover the areas where there aren't any roadblocks."

Rick grabbed his sister's arms and gave her a swift kiss on the forehead. Their cousin Aaron, a deputy sheriff, would understand the urgency, given his family's experiences with the SSU. "You're a genius, Meggie. Thanks."

"Y'all? I think I may have found something." Isabel's voice floated in from the living room.

Rick, Jesse and Megan returned to the other room and joined their siblings around Isabel's computer. "What?" Rick asked.

"This is the back view of the Subaru—from the parking lot camera. What do you see in the back there?" Isabel pointed to a zoomed-in view of the Subaru's back hatch.

"That's a tent," Wade said.

"So he's planning on doing some camping?" Shannon asked.

"Gossamer Mountain," Jesse said. "Best camping spot around here, and Damon spent a little time there year before last when he was on the MacLear SSU team sent after Abby and Luke."

Rick pulled out his phone again and dialed his cousin's

cell phone. Luke answered on the third ring. "What's up, Rick?"

Rick caught him up on the recent events. "We think Damon's taken her up Gossamer Mountain. You were with him when everything went down before—any idea where he'd go?"

"There's a cabin up there—up near the big bluff overlooking the lake—that's where Abby and I stayed while we were hiding from the SSU."

"I know the bluff—there's a cabin there now?"

"Yeah. Jake and Gabe helped Dad build a bunch of cabins on our property in the mountains. You should take the two of them with you. They're the best trackers in the family. Want me to call them?"

Having his cousins along as guides might be a big help, Rick realized. "Have them meet me at the marina." Rick said goodbye and turned to the others. "Jake and Gabe are coming with me."

"We'll come, too," Wade said.

"No." Jesse shook his head. "Too many of us, we might spook the people looking for Amanda. We don't want to stumble into people who have no problem shooting first and asking questions later."

Jesse was right. They needed to keep a low profile until they knew more about what was going on. "I may need y'all to back me up if all hell breaks loose," Rick said.

"You've got us," Jesse said firmly.

Rick looked at his brothers and sisters, an unexpected lump forming in his throat. He hadn't realized just how much he'd missed them while he was roaming the world.

Or how damned much he needed them now.

"I've told them you're staying in the cabin at the top of this bluff." Damon kept his voice low, although so far, they'd seen no sign of any other people in the woods that blanketed Gossamer Mountain.

Amanda peered up the steep slope of the bluff, wondering how on earth she was supposed to get up there in time to help Damon if he needed her. He'd provided her with a small handheld two-way radio—one burst of static would be their signal if he needed her to move in; two bursts meant his plan had worked and she should make herself scarce.

And three bursts would mean get the hell out of Dodge and call the cops.

"You're not going up that slope," she stated flatly. "You'll be a sitting duck."

"No, I'll circle around. I'm going to meet them there and tell them that I've just learned the Coopers moved you only hours ago."

"You really think that's going to convince them you're a valuable man to have on their side?" she muttered. "To me, it sounds more like you're a big screwup."

He shot her a look of annoyance. "I suppose you have a better idea, spygirl?"

She returned the annoyed look. "Yeah. Putting me in the cabin before they arrived and sending in a CIA paramilitary team to take them out when they came after me."

"You know why we can't involve the CIA in this."

She sighed. "You don't even have a guess who's pulling the strings at the CIA? It would have to be someone fairly high up."

"Yeah, that's what Quinn thinks. But we don't have enough evidence to justify siccing a congressional panel on their backsides, so we're just going to have to do it Quinn's way. Do you think you can climb the bluff if necessary?"

She gazed up and assessed her chances. Even with the injury to her arm, she should be able to do it. "Yeah."

Damon started walking away, heading to the east, where the land rose at a less steep angle.

Amanda peered up the slope. Damon was wrong—no way would she be able to reach him in time to be any sort of help to him if she had to start out at the bottom of the slope. She glanced in the direction Damon had gone and saw he'd disappeared from sight, swallowed by the forest's thick spring growth. She looked back up at the top of the bluff at least twenty feet over her head.

Muttering a low profanity, she started climbing the steep face of the rocky bluff, finding handholds in embedded boulders and exposed tree roots. She tried to move as quietly as possible, knowing that if the former SSU agents were already above, near the cabin, a wrong move on her part could bring all kinds of hell raining down on her.

Near the top of the bluff was a shallow ledge that allowed her to stand and take a quick peek over the edge. Easing herself up until her eyes were level with the top of the bluff, she took a quick look around.

The cabin was larger than she expected, two stories high plus a gabled roof that appeared to house a small attic at the top. She could see only the back of the structure, but by craning her head to her left, she could also see along the side of the house to catch a glimpse of a porch railing at the front of the cabin. It looked like a lovely place for a vacation.

She hadn't been on a decent vacation in about a decade.

"WE APPROACH THE CABIN on three sides," Rick told his cousins as they gathered at the base of Gossamer Mountain about a mile south of the cabin where Luke and Abby Cooper, with the help of Damon North, had made a stand against a two-pronged attack from both a brutal drug lord and the SSU agents sent to retrieve evidence Abby's late husband had gathered against them. "Keep a lookout for the SSU agents—there may be more of them than last time, if our experience in Tennessee is anything to go by."

"Aaron's ready to send a dozen deputies for backup," Jake said.

"Kristen, too," Gabe added. His sister-in-law Kristen was a Gossamer Ridge police officer. "She's on our speed dial."

"Right now, I'm most interested in getting to Amanda and getting her out of the line of fire," Rick said. "Dealing with the SSU is secondary."

"Jake and I discussed the best approaches," Gabe said. "I'm going to go up the back way, climbing the bluff."

"He's the better climber," Jake agreed. "I'll come up from the east, and you come from the west. The north approach is too open—the woods there are thinner, since it was cleared out for the access road."

"Okay."

"You remember how to get there?" Gabe asked with a wry grin. "You've been out of Chickasaw County a long time."

"I used to out-track both of your sorry butts when we were kids," Rick shot back with a grin. "You should worry about me showing the two of you up with my hiking skills."

"Okay, phones on low vibrate. Put 'em somewhere you can feel the buzz." Jake waggled his phone and shoved it inside the breast pocket of his camouflage T-shirt. "You got us on speed dial, right?"

"Yep." Rick shoved the phone in his own T-shirt pocket. "I owe you guys."

"Don't talk about debts until we get your girl out of this mess alive," Gabe said seriously. "I know you're worried, but from what Luke tells us about Damon, he's not going to betray her. If he can keep her safe, he will."

Rick wanted to believe Gabe was right. But he wasn't

sure it mattered—even if Damon wanted to keep Amanda safe, there was no way to guarantee he could.

He parted company with his cousins, heading around to approach the cabin from the west. The climb was a gentle slope made a little more difficult by the tangled underbrush that lay like an impenetrable obstacle course across the forest floor. He'd been hiking for what felt like an hour—but turned out to be only ten minutes—when his phone vibrated against his chest.

Hunkering down, he checked the text message from Jake. 3 men in camo. Big guns. Heading W toward target. Lying low. Chk email.

Rick checked his email and found that Jake had emailed a picture taken by the cell phone. His breath caught as he saw how close his cousin must have been to one of the men.

Then his breath hitched again when he recognized the man in the photo as Salvatore Beckett.

He looked around slowly, suddenly feeling like a sitting duck. He saw no movement, but that didn't mean there weren't SSU agents all around him.

He edged closer to the nearest tree and rose, scanning the woods again. No sign of movement. No sounds. Nothing.

He began creeping forward again, one hand settling on the butt of his Walther. The top of the cabin was just visible through the trees about a hundred yards ahead.

Almost there, he thought, pushing forward through the underbrush.

He just hoped it wouldn't be too late.

AMANDA CROUCHED DOWN on the ledge and tucked herself out of sight while she waited for Damon to send her a signal, checking her watch every few minutes to keep from going crazy with the waiting. Around the fifteen-minute mark, she heard a noise.

Coming from below her.

Carefully, she peered over the edge of the narrow ledge where she crouched. About fifteen feet below her, a dark-haired man she didn't recognize was climbing the wall of the bluff at a surprising rate of speed. He looked to be in his early thirties, well-built and muscular. And he was dressed head to toe in woodsy camouflage, blending into his surroundings.

MacLear SSU, she thought, panic rising in her chest. She tried to focus the sudden kick of adrenaline pumping through her, knowing how easily a person's brain could disengage when danger started closing in. Fight or flight—either were good instincts, but which was best?

If she stood her ground and fought, she had a couple of advantages. She was already on a relatively stable perch, her hands free to fire at the man climbing rapidly up the bluff. And she knew he was coming, but so far he'd shown no sign of knowing she was there, focused as he was on where to place his hands and feet. But gunfire would alert anyone lurking nearby that she was there. And she couldn't fire on a man who wasn't about to shoot her first, could she? What if he were nothing more than a recreational climber?

She heard the sound of loose rocks clattering against the stony face of the bluff and dared a quick look down at the climber. He was pressed against the side of the bluff, waiting out a small avalanche of loose rocks cascading downward, pelting him with light blows.

Suddenly, he looked up. He locked gazes with Amanda, his eyes widening with surprise.

She sprang into action, scrambling over the edge of the bluff and rolling to her feet on the grassy back lawn of the cabin. She darted a quick look around to check for signs of any other intruders before dashing to the back door of the cabin.

It was locked, but there was no dead bolt. The lock could be breached easily, and then she could find something to block the door to keep intruders out.

Darting quick looks back and forth between the door and the edge of the bluff, she pulled out her utility knife, found a thin blade and made quick work of the flimsy lock. She slipped inside and closed the door behind her, locking it and looking around desperately for a way to block it.

She found herself inside a small kitchen, with a breakfast nook to her right and the cooking area to her left. Next to the door, a small refrigerator stood, unplugged.

She rounded it and heaved against the appliance as hard as she could. It was lighter than she'd expected, clearly empty. It scraped over about a foot, effectively blocking the back door from easy entry.

She pulled her SIG from her holster and made a quick dash to the front. Fortunately, that door was locked with a dead bolt, which wasn't unbreachable but would pose a bigger problem than the back door had. She made a quick check of the window locks, as well. Glass windows weren't going to pose any real problem for someone who wanted in the house, but at least they'd offer her early warning of intruders.

Keeping an ear out for any sounds of forced entry, she climbed the steps to the second floor, where she found four small bedrooms, all empty, and a pretty good view of the woods on all four sides of the house. She checked the back to see if the man in camouflage had topped the edge of the bluff. He should have been at the top by now, shouldn't he?

She saw nothing. No movement. No sign of anything out of place. Releasing a pent-up breath, she went to the other window in the room to look to the west. The clearing around the cabin extended only twenty yards before it melted into woods. In mid-March, the trees were past the initial budding period, bright green leaves sprouting on every tree that had lost leaves during the winter, making it harder to see movement among the trees.

Harder. But not impossible.

She spotted movement through the trees about fifty yards away. The bright sunlight outside probably created enough reflection on the windows to hide her presence from observers, but she took a step backward anyway, her attention pinned to the men in camouflage moving with predatory grace through the woods.

A faint scraping noise from downstairs made her freeze. It sounded like metal on metal, then a soft creak.

A door opening.

She checked the SIG's clip. Full, and one in the chamber. Moving as slowly as she could, she edged to the doorway of the bedroom and into the narrow hallway.

The sounds from downstairs had ceased, but she could still feel a presence in the house. She didn't dare head down the stairs—they'd creaked a bit on the way up and would almost certainly give away her location.

Her breathing shallow, she edged sideways until she was at the middle of the hallway, close to the stairs. She glanced up at the second set of stairs rising to what she assumed was an attic. Would there be somewhere to hide up there?

A soft creaking footfall below whipped her attention back to her present problem.

Someone was coming up the stairs.

Chapter Seventeen

Amanda edged back down the hallway and slipped inside the first room, scuttling behind the bed for cover. Minimizing her profile, she watched for movement through the sliver of hallway visible from her vantage point.

She saw a boot. A camouflage-clad leg. The barrel of a Walter P99.

Then Rick Cooper's profile.

She released a sigh of relief. Immediately, Rick whipped around the doorway, his gun leveled at her.

"It's me! Don't shoot." She raised her hands, the SIG still clutched in her right one.

Rick lowered his gun, slumping against the door frame and uttering a quiet, heartfelt profanity. He holstered his gun and took a step toward her. "Are you okay?"

"I'm fine, but how did you get in here? This place is surrounded by SSU agents. There are a few men to the west now, too," she warned.

Rick grimaced.

"There are a few to the east, but I came in from the west."

"How'd you get through the front door lock so easily?"

He reached in the pocket of his camouflage jacket and pulled out a key. "My cousins own the place."

"How'd you find me?" She rose and walked around the

bed, tamping down the urge to fling herself into his arms. "I didn't even know where we were going until we got here."

"We weren't sure—"

"We?"

"My cousins Jake and Gabe are out there. Jake's lying low in the woods, keeping an eye on the SSU guys. You've already seen Gabe—he's the one who chased you up the bluff."

She shook her head. "He's lucky I didn't want to make any noise—he could have had a face full of lead."

"You'd shoot first and ask questions later?" He arched one dark eyebrow at her.

"No," she admitted, digging her feet in where she stood to keep from gravitating closer to him. The pull she felt, the overwhelming urge to bury herself in his embrace, was as strong as a riptide.

"We discussed it with Luke, and he thought Damon might bring you here," Rick finished answering her previous question. "Damon and Luke teamed up here, along with Luke's wife, Abby, and took on MacLear."

Good deduction, she thought. "He told me he thought it would be a hiding place the SSU guys would buy—connected to you, at least peripherally, and they'd come across Coopers hiding there before."

"And here you are."

"Well, technically, I was supposed to be staying at the bottom of the bluff, waiting for Damon's signal."

"Where's Damon's backup?" Rick asked. "All we've seen is a small group of SSU agents."

"There is no backup." She told him about Damon's plan. "I'm afraid I've put it in jeopardy by being here, but when I saw someone climbing the bluff—"

"You had to take cover," Rick finished for her, reaching out to brush back a strand of hair that had escaped her ponytail. "You should have waited for me."

She struggled against leaning into his touch. She'd had a bit of time to think while she was waiting for word from Damon. And one thought kept coming back to her, over and over.

She was putting the Coopers in danger, just being here.

She closed her eyes, feeling as if everything she'd been trying to do was spiraling out of control. "We still don't know who's after me or why. I'm hoping Damon can find that out if his plan works, but it could be a while before they trust him."

"But we do know who's after you," Rick said, catching her hand in his. "At least, we're pretty damned sure we do."

"Who?"

"Ever heard of Khalid Mazir?"

She frowned. "No. Should I have?"

"He's a major contender for the presidency of Kaziristan. Son of a martyred democratic leader. Educated in Britain, moderately attractive without being considered a playboy type. Real model citizen."

"Why on earth would he want to kill me?" she asked, completely confused by the description.

"Because," Rick said, pulling out his cell phone and pushing a couple of buttons, "this is what Khalid Mazir looks like." He held up the phone so she could see the display.

The man on the screen smiled back at her, his dark eyes crinkled with mirth. He was, indeed, moderately attractive.

He was also The Tiger, the ruthless terrorist who'd personally overseen almost two weeks of torture inflicted on her in a Kaziri safe house.

"Son of a bitch," she breathed.

Rick tucked the phone back into his T-shirt pocket and stepped forward, pulling her into his arms. "Now that we know who's after you, and why, we're going to get him. I promise."

She pressed her cheek against his chest, stunned by the revelation. "He's Zoli Mazir's son?"

"Yes."

"Zoli was one of the good guys." She felt a chill wash over her, scattering goose bumps. "A real reformer from within the government who wanted true peace and plurality and everything we want to see happen in that part of the world. How could his son have turned out to be such a repressive monster?"

"People get radicalized. We've all seen it before."

Three sharp bursts of static erupted from the two-way radio in her pocket. At nearly the same time, Rick's phone buzzed against her cheek.

Three static bursts meant get the hell out and call in the cavalry. She looked up at Rick, who was looking at his phone with a deep frown. "What is it?" she asked.

"A text from Jake. A crew of seven SSU agents is converging on the cabin."

"We have to get out—"

A crashing noise from downstairs interrupted her, sending another cold shudder down her spine.

"Too late," Rick whispered, locking his gaze with hers. "They're already here."

AFTER LISTENING FOR SEVERAL seconds to make sure his ears weren't deceiving him, Rick pulled out his phone and hit the speed dial number for Gabe. He nodded toward the hallway. "Cover me."

Amanda edged toward the doorway with an answering nod.

Punching in a quick call for help, he hit Send.

"Anything?" he asked, keeping his voice at a whisper.

"Very still downstairs," she answered, her eyes ablaze with adrenaline. As much as he didn't want either of them to be here, facing God only knew what was waiting for them downstairs, he had to admit that Amanda hadn't looked this alive since he'd seen her last in Tablis.

"You love this," he said quietly.

She shot him an odd look. "Oh, yeah, impending death is a big turn-on."

"You never wanted to leave the CIA." It was why she'd agreed to the breakup. Why they both had. Because they'd loved their jobs.

"Kind of a moot point now," she whispered back.

"What if you could get your career back? Would you do it?"

She stared at him as if he'd lost his mind. Hell, maybe he had. "Can we table the career-day discussion until after we get out of this mess?"

The faint sound of footsteps padded slowly up the stairs to the second floor. From Rick's vantage point, it sounded like only one person. Amanda turned to look at him and held up one finger, corroborating his assessment. Two on one—better odds than he could have hoped for.

But why only one person?

The sound of gunfire in the woods outside made him jerk. Amanda looked at him in alarm.

Had the SSU operatives found one of his cousins? Or maybe stumbled onto Damon and shot first before asking any questions?

The footsteps on the stairs receded, and now the noise was downstairs again. Rick heard the front door creak open and footsteps on the wooden slats of the porch outside.

"He's gone, for now," Amanda whispered.

Rick's phone vibrated in his hand. A text message from Jake. SSU firing on position—moving to higher ground. Cavalry on way. He showed the message to Amanda.

"Who's the cavalry?"

"All the Coopers—my brothers and sisters, any of my cousins who are available. Three of my cousins are married to cops who work on the local forces." Jake typed in a rapid reply and sent it. "Most of them know these woods like the backs of their own hands."

"Then we need to go out there and help them," Amanda insisted, already moving toward the door.

He caught her arm, making her wince as his fingers closed around her injured elbow. He loosened the grip. "Sorry. But we sit tight until we know what's going on."

"Stay out of the fight?" Her eyes widened with disbelief.

He pressed his fingertips against her lips. "Come here. Sit down. Keep your eyes and your ears open. I just returned a text to Jake letting him know where we arc and asking him to let us know where he needs us. But for now, we wait."

Reluctance painting her expression, she complied, sitting next to him on the bed. She looked like one raw nerve, quivering and ready to snap, jumping when he laid his hand against the middle of her back.

"I just want this over," she said softly, making a visible effort to relax beneath his comforting touch.

"And then what?"

She shot him another look suggesting he'd lost his mind. "I guess I'll figure that out if I get there."

"When you get there."

"Yeah, whatever."

"Are you leaving me when this is over?" The question came out a lot needier than it had sounded in his head when he first thought to ask it. He pressed his lips together in a flat line, annoyed with himself.

Her eyes narrowed. "I haven't thought past the next few minutes, Rick. I have no idea how to answer that question."

His chest ached. "A simple 'no' would have been nice."

She shook her head. "I have no idea who I am anymore. Or what I want."

"Or who you want."

The look that came knifing his way from her blue eyes stung. "You can't question that I want you. Not after the last couple of days."

"You wanted me before, but you walked away easily enough."

Her forehead creased. "There was nothing easy about it. And I wasn't the only one who walked."

"I know." He rubbed his jaw in frustration. Why wasn't Jake texting him back? Or Gabe? Were they both out of commission?

Were they dead?

"Do you ever wonder what would have happened if we'd just said to hell with our jobs?" she asked quietly, the question catching him by surprise.

"All the time," he admitted.

"And what do you conclude?"

Before he could answer, his cell phone vibrated. "It's from my cousin Aaron." He retrieved the text message. SSU backed up. About to take cover in cabin. Still inside?

"We're about to have unwanted visitors again," Rick murmured as he sent a text in reply.

"How many?"

"I just asked that question, as well as how many of the good guys are out there."

Downstairs, the sound of gunfire picked up and the door crashed open. A barrage of footsteps and raised voices filled the silent void below.

"Okay, baby, showtime." Rick stood and edged his way into the hall. "I'm guessing they'll send at least a couple of guys up here—higher ground will give them an advantage."

"So we take them out."

"If we can. They may not be expecting anyone to be up here, so that could give us the advantage of surprise." He motioned for her to stay where she was while he darted across the stair landing to the two rooms that flanked the stairs to the right. Each of them flattened against the wall, locking gazes across the gap.

I love you, he thought, the realization washing over him like liquid heat. He wished there was time to say the words aloud. But as he'd guessed, footsteps came pounding up the stairs, moving at a fast clip.

He gave a quick nod to Amanda. She nodded back.

The first man stepped onto the landing, already turning toward the hallway where Amanda stood. She greeted him by grabbing the strap of his rifle and hauling him to the ground. He didn't have time to react before she was on top of him, stripping the weapon away and sending it sliding out of reach.

Rick barely had a second to see her take action before a second man came into view. As he turned toward the commotion Amanda and the first intruder were making, Rick grabbed him from behind, slamming him against the wall. He jerked the rifle away before the man could react and shoved the barrel of his Walther against the man's throat.

"Not a word," he growled.

The man wore a black balaclava over his face, but the glittering brown eyes visible through the narrow slit in the mask looked familiar. Those eyes widened as he recognized Rick, as well. He uttered a foul epithet.

Rick's gut tightened. "Salvatore Beckett. I could have gone a lifetime without meeting you again."

"Mutual, Cooper." Beckett tried to struggle against Rick's hold, but for all the older man's burly strength, Rick outweighed him by twenty pounds and his relative youth made him stronger and quicker.

He disarmed Beckett, sliding the rifle out of reach and stripping him of the Glock holstered at the older man's hip. "Check for other weapons," he told Amanda as he pulled out the plastic flex cuffs he'd borrowed from his cousin. Hauling Beckett face-first into the wall, he jerked the man's hands behind him and fastened the cuffs.

Rick glanced over at Amanda. She had twisted the man's arm up behind his back, applying pressure. She looked over her shoulder at Rick. "Got any more of those?" she asked quietly.

He tossed her a spare set of flex cuffs, and she secured the other man.

"All I gotta do is yell," Beckett said with a laugh.

Rick pulled his mask off and shoved the knit hood into Beckett's mouth, pressing his knees hard into the man's groin when he started to twist away.

Across the hall, Amanda gagged her own prisoner with his mask. "Don't suppose you have any duct tape in that pocket?"

"Next best thing." He reached into the survival kit attached to his belt and pulled out a roll of surgical tape, shoving Beckett into the wall again when he started to struggle. He wrapped the tape around Beckett's mouth to secure the gag in place, then tossed the roll to Amanda.

After they'd stripped both men of radios, weapons and anything they could use to get free, they wrapped tape around the men's ankles and hogtied their feet and hands together behind their backs. Depositing them both in the closest bedroom and closing the door, they met each other back in the hallway. Amanda was breathing hard from the exertion, but her eyes lit up with blue fire as she grabbed one of the discarded rifles.

"That," she said in a low, breathless voice, "was bloody amazing."

He bent and gave her a swift, hard kiss. "Welcome back, Tara Brady."

Her lips curved in a brief smile, but the sounds of gunfire coming from downstairs drew their attention back to the danger at hand. Rick grabbed the rifle he'd taken from Beckett and strapped it over his shoulder.

His cell phone vibrated. He checked the text message. This message was from his cousin Aaron. "There are twenty deputies surrounding the house. They've established there are six men in here. We've captured two, but there are still four well-armed, adrenaline-pumped men downstairs."

"How do we even the odds?"

Rick grinned as a memory floated through his mind. "We call a couple more up here," he said in a nasal Brooklyn brogue.

"Wow, where'd that come from?"

"Remember me telling you about working with Salvatore Beckett?" Rick asked, picking up the radio he'd stripped from the former MacLear SSU team leader. "Well, I forgot to tell you that one of the ways my partner and I passed the time while we were watching Amahl Dubrov was to practice mimicking Beckett's accent. I got pretty damned good at it." He thumbed the radio switch. "Need assistance upstairs!"

Amanda crossed the hall again, leveling the procured rifle at the stair landing. Again, her eyes met his across the gap, and this time he said the words aloud. "I love you."

Her eyes widened, her brow furrowing. She shook her head and whispered, "No."

Rick's heart sank, but he didn't have time to dwell on regrets.

More footsteps were pounding up the stairs, heading straight toward them.

Chapter Eighteen

Two more operatives flooded into the zone. Rick grabbed the first one, gripping the extended barrel of the rifle he carried and hauling him around to smack hard into the wall. He ripped the weapon away, but not before the man yelled, "Intruders!"

For the next few seconds, sheer madness prevailed. The second gunman running up the steps, alerted by the commotion and the shout of his compatriot, came in low and ready. He got off two rounds, gouging holes in the drywall down the hall.

Rick couldn't see Amanda. Had she fallen?

He forced his mind back to his own problem, shoving the man he'd grabbed to the floor and disarming him as quickly as he could. No time to gag him, and it was too late, anyway, now that he'd set off the alarm. Behind him, he heard gunfire—rifle shots—and he hauled the man into one of the unoccupied bedrooms.

As his captive tried to knock his feet out from under him, Rick landed two quick blows against the back of the man's neck, stunning him enough to still his struggles. Pulling out more flex cuffs, he quickly cuffed his wrists and ankles together behind the man's back and shoved him into the bedroom closet.

Edging toward the doorway, he whipped his head into the hallway for a quick look.

The gunman who'd taken shots at Amanda lay in the hallway, bleeding from his neck. There was no sign of the other two gunmen from downstairs.

Rick carefully eased out into the hallway. He heard gunfire coming from downstairs—two different guns. The other men had remained downstairs at their stations.

He was careful when he bent and checked the pulse of the fallen man. Even as he did so, the blood pumping from the man's torn throat trickled to nothing as his heart stopped beating.

His own heart in his throat, he rose and crossed the hallway, following a path left by bullet holes until he reached the doorway of the bedroom on his right. The door was closed, but bullet holes ravaged a furrow through the wood, light from the room inside trickling out through the openings and painting a polka-dot pattern of luminance on the door across the hallway.

He opened the door, fear of what he'd find inside stealing his breath. He made it about four inches inside the room before the cold steel of a gun barrel pressed hard against his temple.

He heard a quiet exhalation and the gun fell away. Amanda pulled him inside the room with strong hands and shoved him against the wall. "Status report?"

"One trussed like a turkey in a closet. One dead."

Her expression darkened. "The others?"

"Still downstairs."

She stared up at him for a moment, her furrowed brow reminding him of the look she'd given him just a few short minutes earlier, when he'd told her he loved her. "What are the chances we can get out of this without anybody else dying?"

Slim, he figured. But it was worth a try.

The radio he'd taken from Beckett was still tucked into his jacket pocket. He brought it out and depressed the talk button again. "We have four of your men. You're surrounded. You're not getting out of this alive unless you surrender."

From downstairs, the gunfire ceased briefly before two shots, seconds apart, split the air.

Then silence, as still and endless as a grave.

Rick froze, staring at Amanda.

She gazed back, her eyes narrowing with puzzlement.

The unexpected buzz of Rick's phone in his pocket made him jerk with surprise. He checked the message. It was a single word. Status?

Rick sent an answering text—four men killed or captured, two men status unknown.

The silence resumed, lingering a couple of minutes. Then, noise exploded downstairs—a door slamming open, boots crossing the hardwood floor in noisy clumps, men shouting orders.

"Stand down, Rick!" His cousin Aaron's deep voice came from below. "I'm coming up."

Rick and Amanda eased out of the bedroom into the hallway just as Aaron reached the landing, his weapon at the ready. He lowered the gun as he spotted his cousin. "Murder-suicide downstairs." He glanced at the man lying dead in the hallway. "Where are the others?"

Rick showed him to the rooms where he'd left the three captives. Beckett glared at him with murder in his dark eyes as several of Aaron's deputies hauled them outside.

"We need to get your statements," Aaron told Rick as he and Amanda joined the rest of the crew downstairs. Besides the deputies, Rick saw, several of his cousins and all of his brothers and sisters were there.

Isabel caught sight of him and ran over, throwing her arms around his neck. "Are you okay?"

"Fine now," he said with a grin, turning just in time to catch Shannon as she came flying at him, as well.

Megan just grinned at him from behind her sisters. "Can't take you anywhere without it turning into a shoot-out, can we?"

Jesse stood a few feet away, talking to a man in civilian clothes. The man's back was to Rick, but something about him seemed familiar. Jesse caught Rick's eye and motioned for him to come over.

Rick saw that Amanda was also heading toward his brother and the unknown man, her gaze focused like a laser on the back of the stranger's head. Her expression darkened to a scowl.

When he reached his brother's side and turned to look at the stranger, Rick realized why.

It was Alexander Quinn.

"What the hell do you want?" Rick asked, glaring at the spy. Jesse's hand closed around Rick's arm, but he shrugged it off. "You have a lot of nerve—"

"In five minutes, maybe less, there will be six men from the CIA here to take Amanda in for questioning," Quinn said flatly, ignoring Rick's show of hostility. "That can't happen."

"There really is someone at the CIA involved in this," Amanda said in a soft, strangled voice.

Quinn just looked at her, not affirming her statement. But in his hazel eyes, Rick saw all the confirmation he needed.

"Maddox Heller has a safe house set up for you, just outside of Birmingham. You can be there in a little over an hour. I need you to stay there until Heller himself comes to get you. You'll be meeting with Senator Blackledge, who chairs a subcommittee on foreign relations. You'll tell Senator Blackledge and his subcommittee everything you know about Khalid Mazir."

"Will that be enough to keep her safe?" Rick asked.

"Nothing in life is sure," Quinn answered bluntly. "But she'll be a hell of a lot safer handling matters this way than going off with the CIA." He handed Rick a set of keys. "There's a dark blue Toyota Camry parked down at the main road. Take it and drive to Maddox Heller's house. Your brother will handle the authorities."

Rick looked at Jesse. His older brother nodded.

He felt Amanda's hand close around his. "Let's go," she said urgently.

He twined his fingers through hers and let her lead him into the woods.

THE SAFE HOUSE MADDOX HELLER stashed them in was a small house in Gardendale, a northern suburb of Birmingham. The small split-level home in the middle of a tree-lined neighborhood had a sprawling backyard that would have been perfect for dogs or children.

Amanda had never considered having either. But seeing that big yard stretching out below the back deck, she felt a little sad to see it so empty.

Behind her, Rick stepped onto the deck. "It's getting cold out here. Don't you need a sweater?"

She turned to smile at him. "A sweater? You make me sound old and fragile."

He shrugged off his own jacket and swung it around her shoulders, pulling her closer to him. "You're definitely not old or fragile. But your lips are turning a pretty shade of blue."

She struggled against the overwhelming urge to close the remaining gap between their bodies. From the moment she and Rick headed into the woods to this very moment, there'd been no time to talk about anything but survival.

But Rick had told her he loved her. Sooner or later, he was going to want to talk to her about what he'd said.

And she had no idea how to respond.

"You're avoiding me," he murmured.

"I'm standing right in front of you," she answered in an equally quiet voice.

"And yet, you feel miles away."

She forced her gaze up to meet his. "You want to talk about what you said."

He nodded. "I do."

"What's to say?"

"Well, for starters—why did you say no? No, you don't love me back? Or no, you don't want to hear me say it?"

The vulnerable bravery in his voice made her want to cry. "Did you think telling me you love me will just magically solve all our problems?"

He threaded his fingers through her hair, drawing her closer. "Love's not supposed to solve things, baby."

She made a face. "Then what good is it?"

He bent and kissed her, a slow, sweet, heat-building caress that made her head spin and her heart pound. He finally dragged his lips away from hers and brushed them against her earlobe. "Is that a serious question?"

She curled her fingers in the front of his shirt. "I have so much baggage, Rick—"

"Are you talking about your mother? All her boyfriends? The social services visits and the occasional forays into the foster-care system?"

She stared at him, not sure whether to be impressed or appalled. "How the hell—?"

"You told me your real name, remember? I had Shannon

do some records research for me. She emailed it over that first night we spent at Isabel's."

"I can't believe you did a background check on me." She pushed against his chest.

"I needed to know what else in your background might be a threat against you."

"You should have told me."

"I know. I'm sorry. But we've been keeping secrets from each other far too long."

She stopped pushing at his chest, knowing he was right. Her whole life had been one series of secrets after another. She'd thought that was how she wanted it to be.

But secrets were just another way of hiding from the world. Secrets were a coward's way out, and she was no coward.

Not anymore.

"My mother never told me who my father was," she said aloud, picturing her mother's skittish response the first time she'd asked that question. "I'm not sure she knew. She drank too much, and she slept around too much."

Rick ran his fingers along the curve of her jaw. "You don't have to tell me this if you don't want to."

"I want to. I want you to understand—I want to understand—what made me the way I am." She gazed out at the big, empty backyard. "We never had a backyard. We lived in apartments—lots of them, one after another, because my mom could never keep a job long enough to stay current with the rent at any one place for long."

"Is that how you'd end up in foster care?"

She nodded. "She'd have to give me up for a while until she could get back on her feet and prove to a judge that she could take care of me again. And there was that time she actually shot one of her boyfriends."

"He tried to kill her." At her look, he added, "I told you, I read all the files."

She felt a bittersweet twinge. "I used to think of foster care as vacation. I was so lucky with the families I was placed with. They were good to me, and I was just so grateful for a little stability that I did everything I was asked to do. Then my mom would get herself back together and back to the serial apartments we'd go."

"I couldn't find any records on your mother after you turned eighteen," Rick said quietly. "What happened to her?"

"She witnessed a murder about a year after I left home. From one day to the next, she was just gone. I'm pretty sure she's in witness protection somewhere. I'll probably never see her again." She saw a hint of sadness in Rick's eyes. "It's okay. It's best this way. I can pretend she got her act together and is living a happy, sane life."

His smile looked bittersweet. "I used to do the opposite. Imagine my mom was happy here instead of somewhere else."

He'd never told her much about his family. "Where's your mom?"

"Last I heard, somewhere in Europe. She left when I was about twelve—didn't want to be a mother or the wife of a small-town cop. We see her maybe once a year now."

She looked away from his troubled face. "I was never much more than an afterthought to my mom, either."

He wrapped his arms around her, pulling her closer. "I'm sorry, baby. Nobody should have to live that kind of life. We were lucky because Dad stuck around. And he's a great dad."

"I survived." And she had, hadn't she? She'd faced down a hell far more challenging than life with her irresponsible mother. She'd faced it down and survived. And if she had to face hell again, she'd come out on top, because that was the kind of woman she was.

A woman who'd served her country with honor and strength. Who'd fallen in love with a good man three years ago and, damn it, deserved the chance to spend the rest of her life loving him and being loved in return.

Didn't she?

She smiled up at him suddenly, making his brow crease with suspicion. His look of wariness only made her laugh aloud.

"I love you, too," she said aloud.

"Just like that?" he asked, sounding unconvinced.

"I don't think three years is 'just like that,'" she pointed out, lifting to her toes to kiss the underside of his jaw. "But, while I may be a slow study, once I get the hang of something, I'm damn good at it."

He caught her face between his palms. "Are you sure?"

She nodded. "I'm so tired of running away from things that scare me, Rick. That's not me. I don't know how I ever let myself get that way."

"You've been through so much—"

"It's not just that. I've been running away a lot longer than that. It's why I went to work for the CIA in the first place." She shook her head. "But I'm tired of keeping secrets from people I want to be close to. And I'm tired of pretending I don't need anyone else. I do. I need you." The smile in her voice faded, and she felt the prickle of tears behind her eyes, as if admitting her vulnerability had opened a chink in the wall holding back all the fears, doubts and emotions she'd held in check so ruthlessly over the past few years.

"I need you, too," he admitted, kissing away the tears trickling down her cheeks. "I have no idea what life with me is going to be like, but I'm pretty sure it won't be boring—"

She kissed him hard, letting the heat of desire burn away

the tears of doubt. His arms snaked around her waist, pulling her with him into the house. He stripped off the jacket he'd lent her and started on the buttons of her blouse.

The phone rang, making them both groan.

Rick broke away and picked up the receiver. "Yeah?" He listened for a second, then punched the speaker button on the phone. Maddox Heller's voice came over the line. "Blackledge just called. The hearing's on for tomorrow in D.C. Get packed now—you're flying out tonight on a chartered plane."

Rick hung up and turned to look at Amanda with wry amusement. "Are you getting as sick of government interference as I am?"

With a grin, she crossed to him, sliding her hand slowly up his chest. "Just a few more days. Then the world will know about Khalid Mazir and we can figure out what to do with the rest of our lives."

"Any thoughts on that?" he asked as he walked with her into the bedroom to pack.

"Anywhere you are is fine with me," she said, meaning it.

He stopped in the middle of unzipping his suitcase and turned to her. "Same here, baby." He kissed her, hard, making her toes curl up.

Then they went back to packing.

SENATOR BLACKLEDGE PUT THEM up at the Watergate Hotel. On his own dime, he assured them when they suggested less expensive accommodations. His smile was damn near gleeful, Rick noted, when he met them in the room the night before the hearing.

"I thought this place would be appropriate for a top-secret meeting," he said with a grin. "And I suppose you'd qualify as a whistle-blower, Ms. Caldwell."

"Not exactly," Amanda demurred. "I mean, I can't tell you who the mole in the CIA could be—"

"We'll find out," Blackledge assured her. "Meanwhile, you're saving a struggling Central Asian democracy from electing a terrorist mole as their president. For that, you should be given a Presidential Medal of Freedom—"

"No," Amanda said quickly. "If I could do this anonymously, I would—"

"But you can't." Blackledge looked genuinely sorry for her, Rick noticed, although he wasn't sure he could really trust the old politician's words or actions. Blackledge had been in Washington a long time, and the place had a way of corrupting even the good ones if they stuck around long enough.

"Here's how it will go. You'll testify before the Senate Committee on Foreign Relations. I'm on the committee—so I'll guide you through it. All you have to do is tell the truth. What you went through three years ago and the recent attempt on your life. You can do that, can't you?"

Amanda nodded.

"Okay, then." Blackledge sat back in the chair and looked them over. "You'll want to dress up—look a little more put together than you do now."

Amanda slanted a quick look of amusement at Rick. He stifled a smile and asked Blackledge, "What about Barton Reid? Can we pin any of this on him?"

"Unfortunately, Salvatore Beckett seems to be the only one who knows who hired them, and he's not talking. The others were hired by Beckett, and they only knew that he was paying them well to track down Ms. Caldwell and procure her cooperation."

"Her cooperation? They were trying to kill her." Rick's voice rose in anger.

Amanda closed her hand over his arm. "You don't expect them to admit that, do you?"

"What about the shooting and arson in Thurlow Gap?" Rick asked the senator. "I imagine the locals probably want some answers—"

"They'll get them. I've already discussed the matter with Senator Douglas of Tennessee. He's handling it for you even as we speak." Blackledge stood. "I don't want to be accused of tampering with a witness, so it's time I go."

Rick walked the senator out, then returned to where Amanda stood by the window, gazing at a misty view of the Potomac River. "Soon, the whole Tidal Basin will be lined with blooming cherry blossoms," she said as he wrapped his arms around her waist. She leaned her head back against his shoulder.

"Know what cherry blossoms are good for?" he asked.

"What?"

"Weddings." He kissed the side of her throat.

She turned to look at him, a little frown between her eyes. As she started to argue, he silenced her protest with a kiss.

Sooner or later, baby, you're going to see that we belong together, he thought.

Sooner or later.

He just didn't know how soon.

"YOU ELOPED?" ISABEL STARED at Rick and Amanda in disbelief. "No big Cooper wedding?"

"We're not the big-wedding sort," Amanda said in apology, accepting Isabel's quick kiss and turning to look at Rick. "Besides, I'm pretty sure he got me drunk."

"Liar," Rick said, grinning at her and feeling a rush of sheer joy at the sight of the happiness shining in her blue eyes. "We finished up with the hearing around midday, so we decided to rent a car and drive ourselves home. She's the one who spotted the chapel in the mountains on the drive back and said we should get hitched."

"Luckily, Virginia's licensing laws allow same-day weddings, or he might have had second thoughts and run," Amanda answered with a laugh.

"We need a party!" Isabel said, clapping her hands together. She hurried over to the phone.

"I knew we shouldn't have told her first," Rick murmured, wrapping his arms around his new wife's waist.

"I wouldn't mind a little shindig," Amanda admitted, turning to kiss him. A few mind-reeling seconds later, she drew her head back and looked up at him. "Happy?"

"Delirious," he admitted. "You?"

"Not bad at all," she said with a wry chuckle. "Did you ever get through to Jesse about what we were talking about?"

"Jesse wants to talk to you," Isabel interrupted, holding out the phone.

Rick took the receiver. "Hey, Jesse."

"You always were the impulsive type," Jesse said, though there wasn't a hint of censure in his voice. "Congratulations. Amanda's a remarkable woman."

"Yes, she is," Rick agreed, smiling down at her. She arched her eyebrows in response.

"And as for what you called me about yesterday, yes. We have the budget for it, and I've already seen firsthand what an asset she'll be."

"You're hired," he told Amanda. She grinned back at him, clearly pleased. "She accepts," he told Jesse. "And now, get your butt over here to Isabel's and grab you a few Coopers on the way out. We're having a wedding party!"

He handed the phone back to Isabel and turned back to his wife. "Are you sure you really want in on this? The Coopers can be a rowdy bunch to deal with."

"I'm sure," she said firmly, wrapping her arms around his waist. "But are you sure you really want to work with your wife? That's a whole lot of togetherness…."

He'd already spent three years without her. It had felt like an endless lifetime.

No way on earth he'd ever get enough of her.

"Sounds like a dream job to me," he murmured as he bent to kiss her again.

* * * * *

SUSPENSE

INTRIGUE®

COMING NEXT MONTH
AVAILABLE APRIL 10, 2012

#1341 SON OF A GUN
Big "D" Dads
Joanna Wayne

#1342 SECRET HIDEOUT
Cooper Security
Paula Graves

#1343 MIDWIFE COVER
Cassie Miles

#1344 BABY BREAKOUT
Outlaws
Lisa Childs

#1345 PUREBRED
The McKenna Legacy
Patricia Rosemoor

#1346 RAVEN'S COVE
Jenna Ryan

Taft Bowman knew he'd ruined any chance he'd had for happiness with Laura Pendleton when he drove her away years ago…and into the arms of another man, thousands of miles away. Now she was back, a widow with two small children…and despite himself, he was starting to believe in second chances.

Harlequin Special® Edition® presents a new installment in USA TODAY *bestselling author RaeAnne Thayne's miniseries,* THE COWBOYS OF COLD CREEK.

Enjoy a sneak peek of A COLD CREEK REUNION

Available April 2012 from Harlequin® Special Edition®

A younger woman stood there, and from this distance he had only a strange impression, as though she was somehow standing on an island of calm amid the chaos of the scene, the flashing lights of the emergency vehicles, shouts between his crew members, the excited buzz of the crowd.

And then the woman turned and he just about tripped over a snaking fire hose somebody shouldn't have left there.

Laura.

He froze, and for the first time in fifteen years as a firefighter, he forgot about the incident, his mission, just what the hell he was doing here.

Laura.

Ten years. He hadn't seen her in all that time, since the week before their wedding when she had given him back his ring and left town. Not just town. She had left the whole damn country, as if she couldn't run far enough to

HSEEXP0412

get away from him.

Some part of him desperately wanted to think he had made some kind of mistake. It couldn't be her. That was just some other slender woman with a long sweep of honey-blond hair and big, blue, unforgettable eyes. But no. It was definitely Laura. Sweet and lovely.

Not his.

He was going to have to go over there and talk to her. He didn't want to. He wanted to stand there and pretend he hadn't seen her. But he was the fire chief. He couldn't hide out just because he had a painful history with the daughter of the property owner.

Sometimes he hated his job.

Will Taft and Laura be able to make the years recede…or is the gulf between them too broad to ever cross?

HSEEXP0412